THE MARDI GRAS MURDERS

THE MARDI GRAS MURDERS
A novelization of an original Screenplay
by
Ricardo S. Dubois

Editing: Angela Hooper
Cover design: Kathy Dubois
Back Photo Courtesy: Dwight Moore

THE MARDI GRAS MURDERS

ISBN: 978-0-6151-8220-9

CHAPTER ONE

Derrick Riggs looked down upon the stack of files, which piled his already cluttered desk.

"How did I get into this again?" he asked himself, as he pondered the events that had landed him here in New Orleans.

New Orleans, Louisiana, tourist capital of the south especially around the time of Mardi Gras, and Mardi Gras was just around the corner.

Derrick was not here for Mardi Gras; a much more sinister purpose had brought him here. A purpose he had devoted the last eight years of his life to.

Hailed by many as an expert in tracking, analyzing, and apprehending serial murders, he had become a person in demand whenever a police department suspected a serial murderer.

His expertise had come at a high price, a broken marriage, and a seven-year-old son he rarely saw. The daily stress of trying to get into the mind of a psychotic, had driven him to drink as a way to escape the horrors he was forced to experience. He began to question everything about his existence. He often wondered how such evil could exist, why God allowed it to happen. He never resolved this internal struggle, his only reward for his efforts were constant headaches and nightmares.

Derrick found himself leaning on the bottle more and more. Friends tried to intervene, but they soon realized that he could not be helped until he was ready to be helped.

"I can stop anytime I want!" Derrick would often say to concerned friends, but deep down, he knew, as did those around him, that he was an alcoholic.

Derrick had tried to quit several times, but his resolve was just not there. As a result, his career on the Chicago Police force hung precariously in the balance.

"Getting settled in?" a voice asked in a heavy Cajun accent.

Spinning around to the sound of the unknown voice, Derrick found himself looking into the chest of the biggest man he had seen in quite some time. Derrick slowly began to raise his head upward to see who this towering giant was. Slowly looking up to see a six foot five-inch individual looming down upon him.

"Jimmy James," said the giant, as he extended his hand to Derrick. "Just call me Voodoo," Jimmy continued, and as he smiled wide, a gold tooth showed between his lips.

Voodoo almost looked as though he was dressed for Mardi Gras rather than reporting to work in a police squad. His purple suit glistened as though the material had been interwoven with some sort of shiny substance. His custom tailored shirt was half unbuttoned to expose the many gold chains, that hung from his neck. When looking at Voodoo, you didn't know whether to be entertained or frighten.

"Derrick Riggs," Derrick finally replied, as he grasped Voodoo's large ring-clad hand.

"Pleased to meet you. You're new here, aren't you?" Voodoo asked, sitting on the edge of Derrick's desk, lowering himself to be more on Derrick's eye level.

As he leaned against the desk, the Fleur-de-Lis key fob he had hanging from his pocket caught Derrick's attention. It was silver, with an unusual look

THE MARDI GRAS MURDERS

for a Fleur-de-Lis. Derrick had seen many variations of the Fleur-de-Lis in his time, but this one was just a little different. The petals of the flower were smaller, thinner, more fragile. In fact, looking at Voodoo's fob, some were even bent.

"Yes, I'm out of Chicago. I've come to give y'all a hand with these Mardi Gras Murders," Derrick explained.

Voodoo's expression changed, and Derrick could see the change in his face. The three words had struck fear in Voodoo, but Derrick pressed further.

"You ok, Voodoo?" Derrick asked, as a prelude to his next question. Voodoo still did not respond for what seemed a long while, then finally he spoke as he rose to walk away.

"Mardi Gras murders bad Mojo!" he said,

"You know about these murders?" Derrick asked, trying to glean as much information from Voodoo as possible.

"Voodoo knows nothing about them, and is staying far away," Voodoo concluded, continuing to refer to himself in the first person.

Derrick was a little taken back by Voodoo's reaction to the murders, but then again, he appeared to be a strange sort of character anyway.

Settling down after his encounter with Voodoo, Derrick began to pore over file after file of interviews, investigations, reports, and the photos.

The photos were the most graphic he had seen, and Derrick thought he had seen it all. Looking over a series of photos, that detailed the murder scene of a year ago, something caught his attention. The scene was a bloody one, yet as Derrick looked around the room, he was surprised, that for such a brutal murder, the room was
relatively undisturbed.

THE MARDI GRAS MURDERS

Then there was the body itself. Stretched out across the floor nude, stabbed in the chest, then his testicles removed. Carved in the chest of the body was a cross, with a puncture wound in the center of the cross, which ultimately pieced the heart. On the wall next to the victim, probably written in his own blood, was the word "FAG." In each of the murders, the testicles were removed but were never found at any of the crime scenes. This was information only the police were privy to. Not releasing certain aspects of the evidence, had proven very helpful in the past when police were tying to sort out confessions. It had been Derrick's experience that whenever a high profile case surfaced, there would be a score of would-be confessors trying to get their moment in the spotlight.

Derrick pored over the files looking for a clue, that may have been overlooked. But the investigation had been pretty thorough, with few obvious loose ends that jumped out at him. This left Derrick with no place to start, but he had been there before. He knew he would just have to dig a little deeper, and sooner or later something would break.

Deep down, the reality of what Derrick faced was becoming oh so clear. He had a narrow window of opportunity to catch this killer. The week of Mardi Gras, after that, the killer would fade into the dark recesses of the city streets for another year.

It was early morning now and the office activity began to increase as the office began to fill up with officers getting off duty, and officers just coming to work. Laughing and random conversations elevated the noise level as the officers passed over the night's events to their relief.

Derrick had planned to check in with the captain first, after all, he had requested him for this assignment. Derrick would be temporarily assigned to

THE MARDI GRAS MURDERS

New Orleans to apprehend the serial killer that had plagued the city for years. Then after Mardi Gras, he would return to Chicago; at least that was the plan. He had been on temporary assignments before. He knew how they often develop a life of their own. One thing would lead to another, just one more thing, one more troublesome case. Before he knew it, weeks had turned to months, then years. Derricks hoped that would not be the case here. He wanted to catch this guy then get out of Louisiana. Or at least that was his plan. He had spent much of his life trying to get out of Louisiana; he never thought he would be pulled back so soon.

After meeting with the captain, Derrick planed to visit the site where the murders had been committed. Ironically enough, each murder occurred within the confines of the French Quarter, all within walking distance of the New Orleans Police Department (NOPD).

On the surface, this would seem strange, but within a tightly congested city, and the fact that the Police Department was located on Royal Street right dab in the middle of the French Quarter, it would be hard to do any crime downtown without being close to the Police Headquarters. The proximity of the police station did not really matter when you were dealing with a police force that had been so drastically reduced due to budget cuts. The demands to patrol the city with normal tourism had stretched the department dramatically. During Mardi Gras when crowds surged to thousands, It would be an impossible task if not for the help of reserve officers.

Derrick paused for a moment as he reflected back to a distant memory of his parents, aged by time and a faded memory. His mind pulled up an image of him and his parents on a Mardi Gras parade route, waving as the colorful decorative floats passed by.

THE MARDI GRAS MURDERS

"Throw me something, mister!" his younger self shouted, waving wildly as his father held him high on his shoulders.

Seeing his enthusiastic pleas from a passing float, a drunken rider snatched a fist full of beads, almost losing his balance over the side of the twelve-foot high float as he reached for his throws, narrowly catching himself at the last possible moment, obverting his sprawling to the pavement from his elevated perch. Staggering to his upright position, the man reared back and released his projectile of beads straight toward Derrick. Derrick momentarily closed his eyes, reliving the scene that had taken his eye. As his memory advanced further he saw his father screaming as his light brown jacket gradually became stained with blood. The memory faded just as quickly as it had begun, out of nowhere and returned to the same place.

Across the room, Derrick could see movement in the captains office. It was about nine o'clock now, and the office was alive with activity. Phones were ringing and people were scurrying about from one place to another, each carrying a folder or papers of some kind. Each having a specific destination in mind.

Traversing the gauntlet of people, Derrick moved toward the captain's office, lightly tapping on the door.

"Come on in!" the loud, heavily-laden Cajun voice yelled.

"Derrick Riggs, Sir," Derrick said, trying to make the visit sound official, extending his hand to the captain, who returned the gesture, totally engulfing Derrick's hand in his.

To look at the captain, one could come to a great number of conclusions. Unfortunately, most of them would be wrong. Captain Bob Hebert (pronounced A-bear) was not very impressive at first sight. Neither his appearance, nor the unkempt manner he kept his office

THE MARDI GRAS MURDERS

in instilled the least bit of confidence. However, first impressions can be very deceptive. Bob Hebert had not always been the five-hundred pound mass of humanity that now stood before Derrick. Bob had served on the New Orleans City Police force for over twenty years. In those years, he had served with distinction, having earned several accommodations for bravery. What started Bob's downhill physical descent was nothing so dramatic as being shot on the job. No, what would lay Bob up for months and start the gradual weight increase was knee surgery. After walking a beat for years, the concrete eventually took its toll on his knees. Surgery laid him up for months, and put an accumulated amount of weight on him that he was never able to take off. He returned to work riding a desk, and throughout the years, he was promoted. He now held the highest rank in the Police force.

The captain's unkempt appearance and his consistent butchering of what was supposed to be his primary language, English, only served to reinforce people's first impressions that he was an ignorant slob. As Derrick eyed the half-full box of donuts on the edge of the captain's desk, he reasoned that the captain had little interest in making a change for the better.

Yes, one could really underestimate the captain if you didn't know him. But Derrick knew him.

"It's been a long time," the captain said, as he eyed Derrick hard.

"I see you haven't been pushing away from too many gumbo pots have you," Derrick shot the first volley over the bow, so to speak.

"And how about you?" the captain countered, "You still personally trying to deplete the supply of Scotch in whatever city you find yourself in?"

Derrick's expression dropped; he knew his brother knew about his drinking problem, he had

9

probably even made a phone call or two to Chicago. But to throw it up in his face like that hit him hard. But then again, he reasoned, he started it with the wisecrack about his weight. Looking back, he now remembered how extremely sensitive he was about it.

Derrick had never had a problem with his weight; no matter what he ate, he would gain no weight. Derrick being only the captain's half-brother, his genetic makeup was somewhat different. With only an average height, build, his extremely high metabolism more than accommodated his 'eat anything, anytime' lifestyle, which had become a source of jealousy and envy between them in recent years.

Derrick scampered to regain his composure from his brother's blistering attack

"Well, I'm on the wagon now, Bob, and I'm trying to get it together," Derrick said, lying to his brother in the most convincing tone he could manage.

"We'll, that's something I guess," Bob said, not trying hard to conceal the fact that he did not believe a word he said.

"And I've lost fifty pounds, so I guess we both have something to celebrate," said Bob in a sarcastic tone.

Derrick let the obvious last shot go by, he had nothing to gain by arguing with his brother. He would be leaving soon, and it was his hope to leave on good terms with his brother.

"Have a seat, and close the door," Bob offered, motioning to a chair in front of his desk as he plopped his 300lbs form into his.

"How's Alice and Jimmy?" Bob asked, leaning back in his chair.

"They're fine," Derrick replied, not wanting to reveal to his brother the fact that he had not seen either his wife nor son in months.

THE MARDI GRAS MURDERS

"You missed his birthday," Bob said, reaching for a picture frame that was turned away from Derrick. Removing a photo from the frame, Bob tossed it across his desk toward Derrick. "Here's his most recent picture."

Derrick picked up the photo of his wife and son; his heart sank into a downward spiral that knew no end. He had always wanted to do the best for his family, but his job drove a wedge between them that seemed only to grow over time. Immersing himself into the minds of serial killers couldn't help having some influence on you. Slowly, gradually, he had begun to become more isolated, more withdrawn. The constant fights followed with no end in sight. He could only imagine how it was impacting his son. So more and more often, he would stay later and later at work until he and his wife had become little more than two ships passing in the night. Traveling around the country did not help, any.

Before long, years had passed. Either out of shame or guilt, Derrick had chosen not to keep in contact with his son and wife. In time, his wife divorced him, and remarried. Derrick was glad his son had someone he could count on.

It was during this time that Derrick began to drink more and more. Alcohol helped to burn out the faces of the victims he had seen, he was haunted by the pain they must have endure before their death. He wondered how individuals could be so cruel, or sick. No matter how hard he tried to explain and reason the inhumanity he faced on a daily basis, he could find no comfort. Though alcohol offered some relief, it was only a temporary panacea. It ultimately dragged him downward, like a sinking ship on its journey to the bottom of the ocean. Derrick had not reached the bottom yet though, for the most part, he was still in denial. Still thinking he could control his addiction. He was in a constant state of lies, to others, and most importantly to himself.

Derrick began to get a little teary-eyed, but fought back the emotion.

"I won't show Bob any weakness," Derrick thought,
fighting to keep the emotion at bay.

Derrick began to hand the photo back, but the inscription on the back caught his eye. It read: "Thanks for the present, Uncle Bob. Baseball is around the corner so it will come in handy."

Derrick's emotion quickly shifted gears from sorrow to anger; he tossed the photo toward Bob.

"Why did you bring me here, Bob? You got tired of tormenting the people under you, so you thought you wanted to spread your torment a little closer to home?" Derrick angrily stated.

"Torment?" Bob shouted back, his face reddened, and his breathing more labored. "You're tormented alright; tormented by your guilt!" - Bob said, his voice obviously angry. "You self-righteous prick! You have a wife and kid you hardly see, a mother you never call and a brother who hasn't seen you in ten years! You come back here and all you feel is torment! Well, excuse the hell out of me!"

Derrick remained silent, as the truth of his brother's words just hit home. Every word Bob said was the undeniable truth. What had been the case with his son and wife was also true about Bob and his mom. Through time and distance, he had eventually drifted completely apart.

"But that's not why you're here, Derrick," Bob began to explain. "You have earned a reputation as an individual who can solve the unsolvable serial murders, that's why I requested you from Chicago. We have a

THE MARDI GRAS MURDERS

problem here." Bob paused, as though recalling all the murders that had taken place in the last few years.

"Homo's are being killed in a most bizarre manner, only homo's, and only during Mardi Gras," Derrick interjected, what he already knew.

"They don't teach you how to be politically correct in Chicago? We call them gay down here," Bob explained.

Derrick rolled his eyes and exhaled hard. He had been so inundated with political correctness, it made him sick. In recent years, he had seen good people reprimanded because their choice of words had offended someone. Deep down, Derrick knew that you could take any word in the English language, and if you looked hard enough, you could find someone who was offended by it.

"OK, Bob," "Derrick conceded in a feeble attempt to accommodate his brother. "Gay!"

"That's better," Bob said, eyeing his brother hard. "I need your help to resolve this, it's been going on now for three years. The body count is rising. The current total is nine," Bob explained, trying to emphasis upon his brother the urgency of his assignment. "We have a narrow window here, if we can't catch this guy before Mardi Gras is over, he won't resurface until next year."

"I hear the Gays have a big voting block, you must be getting a lot of heat from mayor," Derrick surmised, he knew that the French Quarter had a pretty large Gay population, and in recent years, they had become very vocal, and politically active. Many believed that it was the gay vote that put the current mayor in office. So, Derrick understood that pressure was being put on Bob.

"I don't know what kind of Mojo you work in Chicago, but I could sure use some down here. I got a gay mayor crawling over every orifice of my body. And the pleasure the little faggot is getting from it, I'm beginning to wonder if it's professional or personal." Bob smiled, then laughed with his brother at the joke he had just made.

"Why, Bob," Derrick challenged his brother. "What happened to all your political correctness?"

Bob just smiled but would not respond to his brother's last remark.

"Some things never change," Derrick thought. "Bob is as homo-phobic as ever. In an evolving world of political correctness and increased tolerance, Bob often stuck out. Many viewed him as a prehistoric enigma of the past, long since gone.

Derrick stood up and started to leave, "Is there anything else, Bob?" Derrick asked, as he reached for the door.

"Oh, Derrick, no one knows you're my brother, let's keep it that way," Bob said, his motivation for concealing Derrick's identity being less than obvious to Derrick.

Derrick surmised that he did not want anyone to have any perception of favoritism. As though Bob would have even been capable of it.

"No problem, "Derrick agreed, "no one would believe you were born to a family anyway." Derrick smiled, returning a joke to Bob to field.

"Wait a sec, before you leave," Bob said, as he picked up the phone and quickly punched out a number.

He did not have to wait long before the person on the other end picked up.

"Mark!" Bob shouted. "Get yourself in my office right now," Bob ordered in an excited tone, then hung up.

Turning to Derrick, Bob began to explain his recent lack of phone etiquette to Derrick.

THE MARDI GRAS MURDERS

"These young hot-shot detectives today," Bob said, pausing momentarily. "You got to make them believe you're the baddest mother on the block."

Within only a few seconds, the young man appeared in the doorway.

"Yes sir!" Mark called out as soon as he arrived. "You called me?" the enthusiastic detective asked.

"Who the hell else sounds like me?" Bob shouted the rhetorical charge, while his head moved back and forth. "I wanted you to meet Derrick Riggs," Bob said, gesturing to his brother.

Mark quickly turned to Derrick, extending his hand. "Mark Broussard," he said, as he shook hands with Derrick.

Mark Broussard was one of the younger, more professional police officers that were recruited some time back in an effort to try to upgrade their image and professionalism. Recruiters turned away from the rough and tough everyday cop, to a more educated type of individual, and Mark fit the profile perfectly. He was a New Orleans local, raised all his life there; he went to school at Louisiana State University where he studied Criminology. He was bright, young, and ambitious. A dangerous combination to most of the officers in the police department, who had settled back and began to wait on retirement. They did not need some hotshot out of the academy trying to get them killed by trying to become an over achiever.

Mark was a rising star, it had only taken him two years to go from the academy to being promoted to detective. It was obvious that there was someone giving him a boost along the way. Being assigned to this case was no accident either. As Derrick would later find out, his brother had gotten specific instructions to have him assigned to the case. Some reasoned a high profile case like this could only catapult him even higher, one thing was sure; if this case could get solved, it definitely would not hurt his career.

As Derrick took Mark's hand, he immediately realized how soft it was as he gripped it. Compounded by the fact that Mark had a very weak handshake, it made Derrick wonder about this new acquaintance.

Momentarily reflecting back to what his father taught him as a boy about handshakes.

"Son, if you're going to take a man's hand," Derrick's father would say, "grasp it firmly, don't squeeze it, but don't' be a dishtowel either."

That's what Derrick felt when he shook hands with Mark. Clammy moist limp hands, did not give him or anyone else a good first impressions of this young detective.

"Mark is going to be working with you on the case," Bob informed Derrick after Mark had entered the room.

"I normally work alone," Derrick countered, but before he could begin to explain all the reason's why, he was cut off by Bob.

"Don't even go there!" Bob said, his voice raised to accentuate his position. "You know how it works, you're from out of town. You will be assigned a local representative."

Derrick knew it was futile to argue with Bob, especially when he had his mind made up.

"Very well," Derrick conceded. "I don't want to start the first day off breaking any of your rules, Bob."

"It's Captain to you, and they're not my rules, they're the department's. We don't like loose cannons on our streets. I don't care if they got a badge or not," Bob said, concluding his statement.

Derrick nodded his understanding to Bob. "We're going to be fine," Derrick said, as he turned to Mark, who nodded his head in agreement.

THE MARDI GRAS MURDERS

"Now both of you get the hell out of my office," Bob ordered, as he once again turned his attention to the jelly donuts on his desk.

Derrick and Mark left the office, gently closing the door behind them.

"Don't let him get to you too bad," Mark said to Derrick, as they walked toward Derrick's temporary desk. "He's like that with everybody."

"So, Mark," Derrick began, as they reached his desk. "You're pretty young to have a gold shield, aren't you?" Derrick questioned.

"I guess it all depends on who you ask," Mark countered. "Some would draw that conclusion," he continued, "but age is not always the prerequisite to knowledge."

"You sound like one of them damn philosophers," said Derrick, beginning to feel a little uneasy about Mark's articulation and apparent education.

"Although Criminology was my major at LSU, I did receive a minor in philosophy," Mark admitted to Derrick.

"LSU," said Derrick, changing, the topic off Mark. "How's their baseball team looking this year?" Derrick asked, he knew the answer already as he was an advent baseball fan. From the majors to college, he could recite stats on players and teams. What he was really trying to do was find some common ground with his new partner.

"I'm sure, I don't know," Mark responded, as he paused for what seemed a long time to Derrick, staring at him with a glazed over look in his eyes. "I don't follow sports," Mark admitted.

"Why doesn't that surprise me," Derrick said, under his breath as he turned to the folders on the desk.

"Excuse me?" Mark injected, having heard just enough to want clarification.

THE MARDI GRAS MURDERS

"Nothing," Derrick replied in a more audible tone, not wanting a confrontation with Mark at such an early stage of them teaming up.

Mark and Derrick began poring over the files. Fat Tuesday was a week away, and people had already begun pouring into the city. There were partygoers from all over the world, all merging upon New Orleans to let their hair down, in an anything goes, no holds barred atmosphere.

Solving homicides is difficult enough under the best of conditions. Put in the mix of Mardi Gras and it quickly transforms the difficult, to the near - impossible.

The last parade had already rolled for the night, but the sound of partygoers could be heard from inside the police station. Shouting and carrying on without a care, each was determined to strangle as much of the Mardi Gras experience out of each and everyday. The highlight of the madness was when the crowds moved to Bourbon Street. Crowds would gather under the overlooking balconies and galleries, to call up to the women overlooking the street.

"Show! Show! Show your tits!" They would call out to the women, most of which were more than willing to accommodate.

It was approaching eleven pm when Derrick and Mark finally decided to call it a night, they agreed to resume the next morning, with clearer heads and a better attitude.

The squad room had settled down somewhat, though still very busy, it was not the madhouse it had been earlier. Derrick had been so engrossed in his work, he had not even noticed the gradual transition. Not taking the time to dwell on it for long, all Derrick wanted now was a shower and a bed.

THE MARDI GRAS MURDERS

"I'll see you tomorrow," Derrick called out to Mark, without turning around as he headed for the door. "Maybe a night-cap will settle me down some," Derrick reasoned. "Just one, and I'm off to bed!" Though his thoughts tried to convince himself, his subconscious knew better. So many times in the past, one drink had turned into ten. "Tonight will be different!" Derrick reasoned. "One drink is all I need." Derrick continued to try to convince himself, but he had been here too many times before.

Derrick exited the police station right into a massive crowd of merry makers, who were beginning to disperse throughout the French Quarter. Derrick maneuvered his way toward the Boar's Breath saloon, rumored to be owned by none other than Clint Eastwood. It was crowded, very crowded, but Derrick managed to push his way to the bar. "Bourbon!" he yelled to the bartender over the music and the noise of the crowd.

THE MARDI GRAS MURDERS

CHAPTER TWO

He watched from the darkness, in a shallow recess of a building. He watched as the mass of humanity filed by. He watched not as another member of the crowd, but as a lioness watches a herd of gazelles seeking to identifying the weak, the vulnerable. Once identified, she will separate it from the herd and ultimately devour it. He too was on the prowl, about to take a victim. His victim would not be a random selection from the crowd, his victim had already been chosen.

He now waited for him to return home. It would be in the privacy of his own home that he would ultimately consume his prey. He watched the crowd to kill time, and for his amusement. The crowd hustled by in a mass of tightly packed people. All trying to experience what they had heard about Bourbon Street. One of the most famous streets in the world, it seemed to be the central gathering point at the conclusion of each parade.

Some revelers were dressed in lavish costumes, others barely had nothing at all. As he watched the mass of people, he was able to quickly identify the homosexuals in the crowd. Some clung to each other, while others actively sought other people like themselves that they could cling to. The whole spectacle turned his stomach. In the past, he had always felt they had the right to live and pursue happiness in whatever

THE MARDI GRAS MURDERS

way they chose, but that was before he was … . His face turned flush red with anger and his mind pushed out the memory of an event he fought so hard to suppress. All year long, it seems he had been able to function, by suppressing the thoughts of the nightmarish events that had transpired three years back. Until Mardi Gras, then the thoughts and feeling he had been able to suppress throughout the year came rushing back. Like the water cascading over the falls, soon he was overwhelmed by the memories of the past. He was not sure if it was because of the strong showing of homosexuals during Mardi Gras. Gays have their own parades, unlike the mainstream parades where a king and queen are selected. The homosexual parades only selected a drag queen.

He was not sure what the catalyst that transformed his mind from a 'live and let live attitude', to a 'Kill! Kill! Kill!' obsession was. He burst from the recess, which had acted as a buffer from the mass of people, and began to push his way through the crowd. Angered now just by the thoughts and memories that would surface this time of year. Roughly pushing his way through the crowd as he progressed farther from the curbs of Bourbon Street, the crowds began to diminish until walking became relatively easy.

He now walked with deliberate steps, for he knew where he was going. It was time for some payback. This scourge on society, which had infested the city he loved, would be eliminated even if he had to do it personally, one at a time. Only a couple of blocks from the river now, he moved through the French Quarter; this was an area that was inhabited by Italians a hundred years ago. Now homosexuals infected the entire area like rats. Three more blocks and he arrived at an area that many would probably consider the armpit of the city. The entire area was in a state of disrepair. Neglect, and time

THE MARDI GRAS MURDERS

had taken its toll on a once beautiful part of the city. Reaching his objective, a small two-story stucco building, the address was displayed on the outside of the four-foot wrought iron gate in front of the apartment.

He scanned the house for any sign of life, there was none. No lights, no movement. His victim had not returned home yet, so he would position himself in a place to wait. It was one fifteen in the morning as he settled down in the comfort and concealment of a dark ally across the street, which still offered a view to the door. Waiting now, his anger and his hatred still ate a fever pitch not having been squelched through time. He viewed himself not as a killer, but an instrument of God on a righteous mission to purge the city of a plaque that had infected it.

As his mind wandered, a man began to approach in the distance. Shrouded in the darkness of the ally, he watched and waited, as the large man walked closer, unaware of the danger that lurked only yards away. If only the victim knew of the evil that awaited him. An evil that would inflict horrors upon him that was beyond his comprehension.

He unlocked the steel gate that offered only a partial state of security from any would-be robber. To him, however, the gate represented security. He had been out on the town, bar-hopping several of the gay bars in the area on his perpetual quest for a soul mate, but unable to find that all elusive individual that would make his life complete. He had moved from his small, Midwest town where he often felt like an outcast.

He had always known deep down, something about him was different. It was not until he was in his teens that he truly came to terms with his sexuality. Trying to explain the fact that he was gay to his parents proved traumatic, to say the least. His mother had cried and his father, a man of few tears, decided to express his disgust with his son by beating him and leaving him unconscious on the floor, lying in his own blood.

Packing the few things he could carry, he left never to look back. Leaving his narrow-minded community and all that he had ever known, he ventured out in search of people like himself. He had heard of large communities where gays were not as ostracized as in other towns. San Francisco and New Orleans were the first two that came to mind. The decision as to which town he would set out to make a life in would not be decided after careful and thoughtful deliberation. Instead, the deciding factor would be determined with a flip of a coin. This is what ultimately brought him to New Orleans. It was ten years ago, and he had never tried to make contact with either of his parents since. In fact, he didn't even know if they were dead or alive. Living and surviving on the streets had hardened him when he first came to the city. He often found himself begging for handouts to survive, or when he was really hungry, he often resorted to prostitution. Through the years, he had been able to create a life for himself with the help of some of the friends he had made along the way. He was no longer living on the streets begging for someone to help him survive one more day. He was now a productive member of society. Proud of who and what he was. Though still not fully fulfilled, he was happier now. He had come to terms with his homosexuality, and had written off those who couldn't accept it. He was starting a new life in New Orleans; a city where anything is possible for anyone.

Pushing his way through the gate, he headed upstairs to his apartment. The exterior steps that ran along-side the house were old, and each step gave every indication that this would be the step that would ultimately bring the entire rickety staircase to a crumbled pile of decayed lumber. But as he had done so many times before, he made it to his apartment door.

In the shadows, he watched; he watched as his prey moved through the gates and up the stairs to his apartment. "It won't be long now," he thought, watching his prey enter the apartment. Light immediately illuminated the upper dwelling, and he knew the time was drawing near. Emerging from the ally, and into the street, he was focused, determined, as though nothing was going to deter him from his mission. Approaching the steps, he slowly, deliberately began his assent to the upstairs apartment. As careful as he was to not make a sound, his victim must have heard or sensed something wrong.

No sooner had he reached the landing, his victim was opening the door. His prey in sight, he reached into his pocket and removed the stun gun, pushing it into his victim in one smooth motion.

Falling back into his apartment with a loud thud, the victim lay shocked and paralyzed by the thousands of volts that had surged through his body.

Entering the apartment, he slowly closed the door behind him. He returned the stun gun to his pocket, reached behind his back and came out with a large butcher knife. "I've got work to take care of," he thought, and he slowly, deliberately, approached his victim, the knife leading the way.

THE MARDI GRAS MURDERS

CHAPTER THREE

Bang! Bang! Bang! The series of strikes continued. Bang! Bang! Bang!

Derrick rolled over onto his back, only now was he able to hear the banging on his door. Getting out of bed, he realized he was fully clothed, and his bed was still made. His head ached, and his thoughts cloudy, he did not remember when he had gotten in, or what he had done last night. Most of the evening was a blur. The last thing he remembered was leaving work and heading to the Boar's Breath for a drink. He was totally blank about anything else that may have transpired the night before. Reaching the door, Derrick threw it open. There in the hall stood Mark.

"Quick! Get yourself together," Mark said, turning Derrick around and following him into the room. "We got another one," Mark told Derrick, who was still trying to shake the last few cobwebs in his head.

"Another what?" Derrick demanded.

"Another Mardi Gras murder!" Mark said, as he entered Derrick's room, closing the door behind him.

Derrick's expression changed immediately. He knew another murder would happen, he just didn't know when.

Quickly composing himself, Derrick and Mark headed out the door.

"How far away is it?" Derrick asked, as they exited the hotel.

THE MARDI GRAS MURDERS

"Just a couple of blocks down the street," Mark explained, as he led the way to the site of the murder.

Derrick and Mark decided to walk, even though the humidity was high, which only made it unbearably New Orleans morning.

As they proceeded down the block, Derrick started perspiring almost immediately, whereas Mark seemed totally unaffected by the heat. Living in Chicago for as long as he had, Derrick had totally lost his acclimation to the humid southern climate.

"Here we are," Mark said, indicating a house with police cars stationed nearby.

Ducking under the police tape, they hastily showed the police their badges, then headed for the steps where a young police officer stopped them.

"I'm Detective Broussard, and this is Detective Riggs," Mark said, taking the lead to introduce themselves as they showed the young officer their badges.

"Yes sir," said the officer, "go right up."

As they negotiated the wooden steps, they squealed loudly and groaned under their unwelcome weight.

"It looks like these steps could fall apart at any time!" Derrick said, carefully negotiating the steps, hoping they would not collapse on him.

As they reached the top of the landing, an officer greeted them.

"I hope you guys are ready for this," the officer said, as he led them into the room. "This is the worst I've ever seen."

They had both smelled it, long before they even saw the crime scene. They had both smelled it before; it was the smell of death.

Crossing the threshold of the apartment, the room was full of activity. A fingerprint man was busily applying his trade, while a photographer was taking photos in a back room. In what appeared to be the living room, a large pool of blood had pooled in the center of the floor. Quickly scanning the room, Derrick spotted blood on the walls as though it had been spattered there. Moving to the rear room, there on the floor was the outstretched mutilated corpse. Everything was the same except the place. Mark's weak stomach could not comprehend what he saw. Becoming ill almost immediately, he raced outside to throw up.

He had seen murder before, but never in such a gross mutilated fashion as what he now encountered.

Derrick walked closer to the body. The bloody corpse still dripped blood, indicating the crime scene was fairly recent. The body was stretched out as before, stripped nude, with the testicles removed. On his chest was carved a cross, which was pierced in the center. On the wall written in blood was the word "FAG." The scene was identical to the photos he had seen of the previous murders. There was no doubt whoever committed this murder was also responsible for the others.

"Any clues so far?" Derrick asked the coroner, who was just finishing up with the body. He already knew the answer, there would be no clues. This guy was smart, very smart. The more Derrick began to immerse himself into this case, the more he began to believe the only way he would apprehend this animal would be by accident.

"Not a one," the coroner responded, visibly disgusted by the whole scene. "A cleaning lady found him early this morning. I tell you, though, look at this room," the coroner continued, "this guy was into some strange stuff."

Looking around the room, Derrick understood what the coroner meant. The room was adorned with

THE MARDI GRAS MURDERS

Voodoo paraphernalia. In the corner was a small altar of some sort.

"Was there a Voodoo connection?" Derrick wondered, but then remembered the other crime scenes did not have such a connection. "I'll have to keep this in the back of my mind for now, see if this surfaces again," he reasoned, as he continued to examine the crime scene.

"Do we have a time of death?" Derrick inquired of the coroner.

"We think the murder happened sometime between twelve and two, according to the body temperature."

"It looks like it's him again," Derrick, said, puzzled on just where to start, or how to proceed. "Do we know anything about the victim?" Derrick asked.

"Yes, his name is James Young, has a rap sheet as a homosexual prostitute, worked at a bar called the Pink Flamingo."

"How do you know all this so soon?" Derrick asked, puzzled by the speed the coroner had gleaned so much information.

"Check stub," the coroner contended, holding up a pink check stub.

"You mind if I take a photo?" Derrick asked, positioning himself next to the body not waiting for a response.

"Not at all," the coroner replied, "but be quick, we're removing him as soon as you're finished."

Derrick quickly snapped a few photos with his camera phone; he planned to compare this crime scene to the picture of the other scenes at the police station. He had access to the crime scene photographer's photos, but they would not be ready for a day or two. In the event he needed to reference a photo, he wanted it to be available.

THE MARDI GRAS MURDERS

Thanking the detectives, Derrick realized there was nothing else to be gained, from remaining at the crime scene any longer. He did, however, have an interesting clue to checkout. Exiting the apartment onto the landing, Derrick saw Mark still hanging over the handrail. He wasn't throwing up anymore, just sort of leaning on the rail.

"How you feeling?" Derrick asked, walking up behind Mark.

"I'll survive," Mark said, pausing then adding, "maybe."

"Do you know where the Pink Flamingo is?" Derrick called back to Mark as he walked down the steps.

"Yes, I do but that's a .... ," Mark's words trailed off as though not knowing how to inform Derrick that it was a popular homosexual bar in the area. He was very cognizant of the way it may have sounded. If there was one thing he never wanted to be branded, it was homophobic, or a bigot.

"Gay bar, I know," Derrick intervened as Mark hesitated. "You and I are going there."

THE MARDI GRAS MURDERS

CHAPTER FOUR

"But ...?" Mark said, puzzled at why Derrick would want to go there. He thought about protesting in an effort to obtain more information, but he pretty much knew it wouldn't do a whole lot of good. Besides, he was still trying to get a feel of Derrick. Mark knew some of Derrick's background, but not a whole lot. The little he had been able to pickup from Derrick was that he was abrasive, rude, and obnoxious. These were the more obvious surface traits that Mark had been able to pickup. The more subtle, less obvious was the fact that Derrick did not like working with a partner. It was obvious to Mark that Derrick had pretty much always worked alone. Mark was sure that Derrick considered him a hindrance that he was stuck with.

Derrick led the way out the gate, followed by Mark, who began to close the gate behind him. As Mark closed the gate, the address numbers that were clearly posted caught Derrick's attention.

"Something about these numbers," Derrick thought, as he stared at the numbers. The number thirty-three was posted on the gate.

"What's the matter?" Mark asked, as he stopped to wait on Derrick.

Derrick's attention was once again pulled away from the gate and back into the moment.

"Oh nothing," Derrick said, as he walked up to Mark. "I thought I saw something."

"Well, did you? Or didn't you?" Mark pressed, trying to pry his way into Derrick's head.

"Don't know yet, I'll let you know," Derrick answered as he and Mark continued down the street.

As they came to the corner, Derrick glanced up at the street sign, which had momentarily captured his attention, hesitating for a moment. The corner street sign read, Rue Conti, and Rue Bourbon.

Seeing Derrick's hesitation once more, Mark once again tried to understand what was preoccupying Derrick.

"What do you see?" Mark asked, already knowing that Derrick would not be too forthcoming with information.

"Conti, begins with a C," Derrick said out loud, then walked away from the sign.

Mark hung back, not believing what he had just heard. "This is our hotshot genius," he thought. "Conti, begins with C."

Derrick made a mental footnote of the two events that had jumped out at him. First, the numbers on the gate, then Conti Street. Something was bothering him. Something rolling around in his head, unable to come to a stop. Derrick would revisit it later, but for now, he had to focus on following up on his clue. The check stub from the Pink Flamingo.

"Lead the way," Derrick said, turning to Mark, who had been content to follow behind him.

"Lead where?" Mark asked, having momentarily forgotten about Derrick's inquires of the Pink Flamingo.

"Pink Flamingo?" Derrick said, somewhat annoyed that Mark did not remember.

"You know, you're all over the place," Mark said, becoming annoyed by Derrick's inability or reluctance to communicate with him. "Gates, signs, I can't keep up! You're like a pinball!"

THE MARDI GRAS MURDERS

Derrick heard Mark's frustration, he knew Mark was right. He did have issues when it came to working with others. If it was up to him, he wouldn't have a partner, but it was the Captain's orders and he was going to have to make the best of it.

"I'm sorry," Derrick apologized. "My head goes in a lot of different directions sometimes. I'll try to be more focused."

"Ok," Mark said, satisfied by Derrick's apology. "The Pink Flamingo is on the corner of Bourbon and St. Ann Street. About four blocks away."

Mark and Derrick maneuvered their way through the early morning Mardi Gras crowds. Many of the partygoers were dressed in costume, while others were more content to observe Mardi Gras and not participate to any great extent. There was no shortage of nudity as they walked by a couple of balconies with women showing their breasts in response to the calls of the crowd below.

The Pink Flamingo was well known by the locals as a Gay bar, but it was like so many things in New Orleans. The more bizarre or outrageous it was, it seemed the more it blended in to the flavor of the city. The Pink Flamingo was a two-story pink stucco building, dating back to the eighteen hundreds. If you thought the gays wanted to keep a low profile in the city, the bright pink building removed any hope of that.

As they entered the dimly lit building, the first thing to grab Derrick's attention was the smell of cheap perfume. Not only was it cheap, it also permeated an overwhelming presence throughout the building. Derrick had never liked strong aromas. Even when he was married, he often cautioned his wife about excessive perfume.

But now he was forced to endure this putrid smell in order to find out what he could about the victim.

THE MARDI GRAS MURDERS

Derrick walked up to the bar and waited. Before long, a young lady of about twenty-one approached them. She was truly a sight. Blond hair was sticking straight up, much like the famous promoter, Don King. It was not until she spoke with a harsh raspy voice that Derrick realized his initial assumption that she was a female was entirely wrong.

"What you guys have?" he asked, eying Mark real hard. "Do I know you?" the bartender asked, directing his question to Mark.

"I don't think so, why do you ask?" Mark questioned, in response to the surprising question.

"You look familiar, that's all," the bartender explained.

Mark shook his head and shrugged his shoulders, not knowing what else to say to the bartender.

"I'll have a coke and some information," Derrick said, as he reached into his pocket for his cell phone. He flipped open the cover and began pressing a series of buttons until he found what he was looking for.

Showing the picture he had taken earlier of the victim, Derrick handed his cell phone to the bartender.

"Do you know this gentleman?" Derrick asked, as the bartender took the cell phone and looked at the photo. His facial expression changed in recognition of the man in the photo.

"My god!" the bartender said, shocked by the image of the photo. "It looks like Liza! He works here, ... ah, he did," he said, refining his earlier answer. "What happened to him?"

"He was murdered," Derrick explained. The bartender repeated Derrick's words, unable to believe what he had just heard.

"Murdered! But I just saw him yesterday." The bartender offered, unable to believe what he heard. "Who would do such a thing?" he questioned."

THE MARDI GRAS MURDERS

"We were hoping you might be able to help us with that," Derrick replied. "Do you know anyone Liza had contact with that seemed a little peculiar or out of place."

"Honey, everyone who comes in here is peculiar in one way or another," the bartender explained.

"Do you know of anyone giving him any kind of trouble in the last few days?" Derrick inquired further.

"No not really," the bartender began, "but Liza had a way of staying in trouble a lot. The police liked to hassle him because he was so big. It made them feel powerful, I guess, to hassle a queen the size of Liza, when they knew he couldn't fight back."

Taking a moment to ponder the bartender's words, he wondered if a police officer could be involved. After all, it was not unheard of. Officers work with the dregs of society on a daily basis. Sometimes the daily grind of arresting criminals only to see the judicial system release them becomes more than some can take, and they snap. Becoming one-man vigilantes. This would be the worst possible scenario for Derrick, and he knew it. A cop knows the in's and out's of an investigation. This means he knows what to do, and most importantly, knows what not to do. If there was a cop involved in these murders, the difficulty of Derrick's task had just been compounded.

"Was there ever a specific officer, or group giving him trouble?" Derrick asked, trying to narrow down who might have had it in for Liza.

"He never went into detail," the bartender explained, "just generalities."

Derrick knew he would get little more from the bartender, and decided to break off the interview for now.

THE MARDI GRAS MURDERS

"Thank you for your time," Derrick said, handing the bartender one of his cards, which had been altered to reflect his New Orleans phone number.

"Chicago Police Department?" commented the bartender. "What you doing way down here?"

"Working on finding Liza's killer," Derrick countered, not willing to go into great detail about his assignment.

"Ok, sweetie," the bartended said, as he winked at Derrick. "If I remember anything, I'll let you know."

Exiting the bar, Derrick and Mark paused for a moment on the corner, as Derrick removed a cigar from his pocket and lit it. Derrick sensed Mark was anxious about something, but didn't quite know what it was, so he prodded his new partner, trying to understand what was making him so uncomfortable.

"You act as though you're in a hurry to leave?" Derrick said, as he puffed on his cigar.

"Can we go now?" Mark pleaded, looking around as though looking for someone.

"What's your hurry? Derrick questioned, "Take a moment to smell the magnolias, and have a cigar," Derrick said handing Mark a cigar.

"I don't want a cigar," Mark said, refusing the cigar. "I also don't want someone I know to pass by and see us coming out of this place."

"Oh!" Derrick said, in a half laugh. "You're homophobic!"

"I'm not!" Mark objected, "I just don't want anyone getting the wrong idea."

Derrick just smiled and continued to take long drags on his cigar.

"Don't worry sweetie, your secret is safe with me." Derrick put his arm around Mark.

THE MARDI GRAS MURDERS

"Cut it out! That's not funny!" Mark firmly corrected his new partner, pulling away at the same time.

"What now?" Mark asked, anxious to move to the next phase of the investigation.

"We wait for lab report for now, hopefully we get a break," Derrick explained

In the distance, a band could be heard leading a parade that had just started. The morning was hot and the sun was shining, too beautiful a day for working on such an ugly business.

The two detectives began walking down the street, headed toward the police station, which was several blocks away. Mark viewed it as a good opportunity to try to crack into Derrick's impermeable facade.

"Well, tell me a little about yourself," Mark asked as he walked with Derrick. "You said you were from Chicago originally?"

Derrick eyed Mark hard, not knowing for sure if his motives were as innocent as he tried to make them seem.

"I'm from a lot of places," Derrick said, pausing for a moment as he prepared to deliver a verbal punch he knew would make Mark extremely angry. "But do you know what the one thing all these places had in common?" Derrick asked, drawing his unsuspecting partner in.

"No," Mark said, taking the bait.

"They all mined their own business," Derrick said, stopping to look Mark square in the eye.

Mark was visibly taken aback by Derrick's remark. He did not quite know how to respond, it was as though he had been hit in the chest with a sledgehammer.

"Sorry," Mark eventually responded. "I was just trying to be friendly."

THE MARDI GRAS MURDERS

"I'm not down here to make friends!" Derrick said, determined to establish the ground rules with Mark once and for all. What's the worst that could happen? He wouldn't want to work with him? That was fine with Derrick; he wanted to work alone anyway. "If I need a friend, I'll buy a dog."

"He'd probably just bite you!" Mark snapped back, no longer willing to take any more crap off Derrick. "You're an asshole, and you're on your own, I'm not taking anymore crap off you!" Mark said, then turned, and walked away.

Standing on the corner, he watched Mark walk off. "The boy's got a set," he thought, then started back toward the station to check on the lab reports.

The crowds had already started to gather in the streets, drinking, carousing, with some pushing the envelope that would determine if they would stay on the street or land behind bars.

Walking through the front doors of the police station, Derrick knew it had been a busy night in the city. The room was crowded, with several individuals being processed for disorderly conduct. Derrick knew the infractions must have been somewhat serious in nature, because during Mardi Gras the police often turned a blind eye to what any other time of year would constitute an arrestable offence.

Derrick reached his desk and tossed his note pad down on top of some of the other papers that scattered his desk. On his lap was a post note he had written earlier. *"Get lab report."*

Sitting at his desk, he began to organize in his mind the task he was going to try to accomplish today. He was going to go to the lab first, that was a no brainier. He wanted to see if the lab was able to produce an additional lead for him. Next, he wanted to go back

THE MARDI GRAS MURDERS

to Liza's house to see if he could find any additional information.

Derrick was beginning to grasp at straws, but if he could get something, anything started, maybe one lead would point to another, and so on. Looking down at his note pad, Derrick saw Liza's address jotted down. This triggered the mental note he had made earlier, when he left Liza's and he was on Conti Street.

Picking up the stack of files that reference the previous murders Derrick realized each address started with a three, then the next two letters corresponded to the day of the murder. "My God!" Derrick thought. "There's a pattern after all!" Derrick wrote down the street name Conti. He wrote it again. "Conti!" Derrick said out loud, his facial expressed dropped as he remembered the name of the parade that had rolled the night before, "Cornelius!"

"I've got it!" Derrick thought, struggling to contain his excitement. He had broken a hidden code the killer had put in place. It was there the whole time, as though taunting him to figure out the hidden clues he had placed in his path. As though engaging him in some sort of twisted cat and mouse game.

"I've broken part of the code!" Derrick thought excitedly. "The killer targets gays that live on streets with the same letters that match the parade that is rolling!"

Having a piece of a still fragmented puzzle, Derrick began to think how he could spring a trap for this guy.

"The streets in the French Quarter are long, how could we possibly watch every house?" he wondered.

Derrick knew he would have to get inside this killer's head, finding this clue had just opened the door.

It was about mid-morning now as Derrick's stomach began to growl. Reaching into his jacket pocket, he removed a flask for a celebratory drink. Leaning low behind the desk, which he hoped would partially conceal him, Derrick downed what was left in the flask. "So much for breakfast," he thought.

Reaching for the phone, Derrick dialed the lab. A soft gentle voice on the other end of the line said, "Hello."

"Hello," answered Derrick. "This is Detective Derrick Riggs."

"Yes, Detective, how can I help you," she said, in her most professional manner.

"I'm calling to find out if you have the lab reports ready for the homicide that occurred this morning?" Derrick questioned.

"Ready?" she laughed. "I just got them, they won't be ready until tomorrow."

"Tomorrow!" Derrick exclaimed, disappointed by the delay that had been imposed on him. "Is that the best we can do?"

"Yes, we're pretty backed up down here," she said, then waited for the response she knew was inevitable. She was always being rushed; everybody was in a hurry with everyone's work taking priority over the other. She had been screamed at, cursed at, and called every name under the sun. She understood the amount of pressure the officers, and the prosecutor's office was under. Over time, she had toughened up, able to take a stand and hold it firmly, no matter how much she was pushed and rushed. She would perform her job in the most efficient competent manner she could. Nothing more, nothing less.

Derrick, however, would surprise this up to now unknown lab person, with a different approach. One that if ever used, she could not remember when.

"I'm sorry," said Derrick, "I didn't get your name."

THE MARDI GRAS MURDERS

"My name is Lena," she replied, her tone harsher, more cautious. "You can report me all you want, but you're still not getting your lab work until tomorrow," she said, misinterpreting Derrick's motivation for the question.

"Report you!" Derrick said, surprised by her response. "Why would I report you, you're just doing your job."

Whether it was the words or the tone in which they were delivered, but something struck a chord inside of Lena. Her defensive shields began to lower as she began to become more receptive to Derrick.

"Lena, that's a pretty name," Derrick said, as he began to sweet talk Lena.

"Thank you," Lena said cautiously, she suspected Derrick was up to something, and she pretty much knew what it was. But there was "something about him," she thought that may require further examination.

"Lena, Can I be frank with you?" Derrick asked, his charm starting to ooze.

"Sure," Lena said, "I love frankness."

"I'm in an awful bind for the lab work, is there anything we could do to expedite it a little sooner?" Derrick asked, his tone soft, vulnerable.

"We would have to put it ahead of other work," she replied, but sensing Derrick's pleading tone, she chose to ally him. "Call me back this afternoon. I'll see what I can do."

"Better yet, Lena, I'll come by personally to thank you," Derrick said, the inflection of his voice excited. "I'll see you this afternoon, around five." Derrick hung up the phone before Lena could respond.

"But ....," Lena said, but never got a chance to deter Derrick from coming. Now she almost felt obliged to have the results ready. She wondered if that's what he had in mind all along.

No sooner had Derrick hung up the phone than he looked up to see his brother signaling him to come to his office.

"You want me?" Derrick asked, as he entered the captain's office.

"I need for you to go to this address this afternoon," Bob said, handing Derrick a folded piece of paper.

"Is this a lead?" he asked, without looking at the address.

"No," Bob said, returning to his seat behind his desk. "It's an obligation."

Derrick left Bob's office and slowly unfold the piece of paper, almost knowing what it was before he read it. Scribbled on the note was an address and a phone number. Derrick recognized it as his mother's address.

"I do need to see her," Derrick reasoned, yet he was not up for all the questions that would surely follow about his marriage breaking up.

"Too much stress," Derrick thought, reaching for his flask.

Only then did he realize it was empty. "I need a drink," he thought. "Just one, to take the edge off, then I'll be fine," he thought, trying to convince himself that it was true, but knowing deep down it would take a lot more than one.

Derrick headed out of the police station and out into the warm midday air. The sky was clear and there was music in the streets, as the crowds of people began to gather for another day of festivities. "Mardi Gras," Derrick thought. Two words known throughout the world for one continuous party. The words Mardi Gras were French, meaning Tuesday Fat, or Fat Tuesday.

THE MARDI GRAS MURDERS

This represented the day before Ash Wednesday, which marked the start of the Lent season. Derrick always had a problem reasoning how the word Gras began to be used.

Tradition ran deep in this metropolitan melting pot known as New Orleans, a city of predominately Catholic influence, yet host to a diverse cultural representation.

Derrick did not care about that now though, all he wanted was a drink.

"I need a drink," he thought as he walked toward Jackson Square. "I need to think, and if I have a drink, I can relax and think better," he reasoned.

THE MARDI GRAS MURDERS

CHAPTER FIVE

Derrick soon arrived at a corner bar across from the Farmers Market. It was a hole in the wall dive with few patrons, especially during this part of the day. The bar was dark, which appealed to Derrick. The only light illuminating the area was from a small TV positioned behind the bar. It was unclear exactly how old the bar was; it had probably been in operation for many years if the smell of old beer on the floor was any indication.

"What'll you have?" the bartender asked.

His eyes not quite adjusted to the darkness, he recognized the voice as being that of a woman. As his eyes began to adjust, he was a little surprised at how pretty a woman she was for being in such a hole in the wall dive.

The middle-aged beauty, revealed few indicators that could ultimately show her true age. Shapely and slim, with large firm breasts, which Derrick could not immediately determine if they were real or not.

Derrick resisted his first impulse to stare at her breasts. He knew a woman like her had been stared at a lot. He knew most men who came into the bar did not know the color of her eyes. Realistically, Derrick could care less what color eyes she had. But since he was going to be here a while, he reasoned, he might as well make a good impression.

The woman smiled, over the years she had become accustomed to men staring at her breasts. She had become so accustomed to it that it hardly fazed her any longer. What did get her attention, and made her take notice was the fact that Derrick did not. He looked her in the eyes.

"Bourbon," Derrick said, as he slid onto a barstool. As he looked around, he realized he was the only one in the bar.

Derrick would settle down on a stool to nurse a few drinks, and think about the case. The bartender, though curious, did not press him for conversation.

As he sipped his whiskey, he thought about solving the case and getting back home to Chicago. "What am I in such a hurry to get back to?" he began to wonder, as he downed a double shot, motioning to the bartender for another.

As the bartender was retrieving his drink, his attention was diverted to the television behind the bar.

"In local news today, the Mardi Gras Murders continue," the reporter began. *"Sources close to the investigation report a serial killer expert from Chicago has been brought in to help with the investigation."*

Derrick's attention was peaked! "Surely they won't release my name, he thought, as the reporter continued.

"The expert's name has not been released, but the news of enlisting outside help is providing little comfort to the gay community who has been the target of these crimes."

The camera pulled away, revealing a tall broad-shouldered man dressed in drag. "I have with me Gina, a spokesperson for French Quarter Gay Rights Movement. Gina, what do you think about the expert from Chicago the NOPD has brought in?"

"It's about time!" Gina said, the deep raspy voice removing any remaining doubt of his sexuality. *"If it had been straights or tourists being killed down here, the*

THE MARDI GRAS MURDERS

police would have been all over it. But since it's just us queers, they've been dragging their feet."

The camera zoomed back in on the reporter, who was closing out the segment. "There you have it, reaction from the Quarter, back to you."

The TV cuts back to the studio and continued the news reporting on the day's parades.

As the bartender returned with his drink, he began to nurse it and ponder, first the case, then his life.

His wife Sally had left him without so much as a note. She went back home to Seattle with his son in tow. Derrick's mind drifted back to a better time, a time when he and his wife were happy. A time when he didn't drink, and would go home at night. He had met her at a convention in Dallas, a convention he had only decided at the last minute to attend. All the weapons manufactures and police supply companies would meet to show off the latest and greatest in law enforcement equipment. The convention was a huge display; everything from small arms to small tanks.

Sally was working at a booth that manufactured Mace. Derrick was infatuated with her immediately, and spent pretty much the rest of the convention pursuing her.

She was not an easy catch he recalled, she had turned him down several times before his persistence finally paid off and she relented, agreeing to have dinner with him. In time, he was able to melt away her defenses with his overwhelming persistent charm. In what seemed no time at all, they were married. He remembered how he had invited the whole family to Seattle for the wedding, but not a single person showed, not even his mother. The pain and resentment he harbored for his family for not showing up at his wedding was one he would harbor for many years. "I had invited my whole family but none were able to attend," he thought.

Taking his family not attending his wedding as a personal rejection, he distanced himself from everyone. Thus straining already strained relationships.

Derrick remembered how his mom and Bob always sent cards on special occasions and holidays. An outreaching act of kindness and love he chose not to reciprocate.

Derrick recalled the birth of his son, one year latter. There is no greater gift from God than for a man to hold his son. Derrick recalled how he felt the first time he held his son; the joy, pride, and emotion that swelled up inside of him.

But with the birth of his son came greater responsibilities. He was now driven to succeed. Not only for himself, but for the family. After working so hard for so long, he realized he was just absorbed into his work. He could not totally recall an exact moment that he could point to and say, this was the turning point. It was more obscure, more gradual, but all the same, it was total. He never blamed Sally for leaving him. He knew it was the best thing to do for their son, and for her.

She saw Derrick had a problem that would only get worse if he didn't get help. But help, was the farthest thing from Derrick's mind. No matter how many times Sally brought up the subject, he would not agree. Sally knew, as did he; a person must first want to be helped.

"God, how I missed them!" Derrick thought as he downed another shot of whiskey. "I had a job to do and it was an important one!" He would often reason, justifying not seeing his son more. "I was the chief detective in a high profile serial killer case in Chicago. Lots of coverage, both radio and TV."

THE MARDI GRAS MURDERS

Derrick ultimately caught the killer, who the media had nicknamed, *"The Butcher of Chicago."* A serial killer who mutilated stranded motorist in the Chicago area. It was a case that brought him fame; he was featured in all the local as well as national news broadcasts. He was the man who caught the Butcher of Chicago.

The secret to his success was really no secret at all. It was pure luck, and hours and hours of driving back roads. Writing down the license plates of all unoccupied vehicles he would come across. After a tip from a passing motorist, who saw one of the victims getting into a car that they were able to give a description off, he was able to match the description with one of the cars he had noticed parked on an isolated road. After a search warrant and countless hours of lab work, he was able to say conclusively, "We have our killer!"

Branded a hero, he began to handle special cases. The hard to solve cases, which suggested they might in some way be connected to a serial killer.

This began his obsession and success. When Derrick was able to apprehend another serial killer, the next thing he knew, he was being refereed to as an expert on the subject. Not long after this, Derrick was bombarded by various law enforcement agency seeking his help and advice. Along with success and fame came the constant pressure to succeed.

It started off slow, he recalled, an occasional drink on the way home. Then the occasional stop at the bar on the way home. Until gradually, it was an everyday ritual to stop at the bar on the way home. His celebrity status had insulated him for a time, until it's worsening effects could no longer be ignored.

THE MARDI GRAS MURDERS

Derrick remembered when his captain sat him down and said he was lending him to New Orleans for a period of time.

"Please Derrick! Get it together down there, or don't come back," his captain had told him. It was like a knife had totally eviscerated him, spilling his guts on the floor for all to see. He had always admired his captain and they had become close friends over the years. Looking back, Derrick now realized how much his captain had covered for him, and overlooked so much. At the time, he was angry. How dare he threaten to fire the man who took serial killers off the street? They say hindsight is twenty-twenty, and looking back now with a clear perspective, Derrick saw what a friend his captain had been to him.

"If I can get my act together," Derrick reasoned, "I'm sure the captain would want me back." If getting himself together was the ultimate goal of his banishment, Derrick was no closer now than he had been when he left.

Derrick knew he would have to solve this case. This is what he had to focus on now. Not the fact that he would have to sober up. He did not seriously consider that option. He believed if he solved the case, everything would be all right.

Still remaining in denial, Derrick never was able to fully appreciate the real reason his captain sent him to New Orleans; that being he did not want his friends and co-workers see him self-destruct.

Derrick downed another shot of whiskey and began to once again focus on the case. He recalled the Voodoo paraphernalia that was found at of the last of the murder scene. "The photos he had been studying did not show any Voodoo alters or paraphernalia." He reasoned but began to think outside the box. "Was this some kind of occult ritual?" he wondered. "Some bizarre sacrifice that could only happen during Mardi Gras?" Derrick reasoned. "If this was a Voodoo ritual, there's only one place to go for the answers to Voodoo," Derrick thought, as he threw back his last shot of bourbon.

Tipping the barmaid, Derrick slid off the bar stool and headed out the door into the midday sun, which momentarily blinded him. Adapting to the brightness, Derrick set his course for his new objective, ... Bourbon Street!

Madam Laveau's Voodoo shop had been a New Orleans landmark for as long as anyone could remember. If there was anything anyone wanted to know about Voodoo or the occult, Madam Laveau's was the place to go.

Standing outside the gray wood structure, on the corner of Bourbon and, Orleans Avenue, an eerie, uneasy feeling came over Derrick. Although Derrick never put a whole lot of faith in Voodoo, he did respect what he didn't understand enough to keep his distance.

Marie Laveau's Voodoo shop was named for the most famous of all Voodoo Queens, Marie Laveau. During the 1800's, few people were sought out more than Marie. From matters of love or a good old-fashioned curse, everyone from the working stiffs, to the elite of society. They all sought out Marie, at one time or another.

As Derrick entered the shop, he immediately smelled the heavy incense that covered the entire shop. The wooden floor creaked with each step he took, as though trying to warn of the eminent danger he faced if he proceeded on. Passing the altar of Marie Laveau, where her portrait hung, surrounded by skulls, branches, feathers and a table to cast a coin to bring luck or help cast a curse. Staring at her picture it was as though her cold, emotionless eyes could pierce your very soul, as it watched your every step inside her shop.

THE MARDI GRAS MURDERS

Regardless of where you stood in the shop, Marie Laveau's eyes were on you. On the opposite wall were charms and potions for any occasion. The shop had become very popular with tourists, and the shop was more than willing to accommodate them by offering souvenirs and charms to fit any occasion. The heavy smell of incenses which permeated the entire building also served a purpose as subtle and mundane as the potential power of the potions and curses. It masked the unmistakable smell of marijuana.

Emerging through a curtain of hanging beads, a dark gothic-dressed black woman emerged from the back room.

"Con I hep you, mon?" she asked in a soft seductive Jamaican accent.

"Yes, I'm looking for Madam Thibodaux?" Derrick asked, politely.

The woman's face changed expressions immediately, as though she had seen a ghost!

"Don't know notin about no witch!" she stated flatly, with a slight quiver in her voice.

"I didn't say she was a witch, did I?" Derrick countered, removing his badge at this point and holding it right in front of the woman's face. "See this," Derrick said, showing her the badge then returning it to his pocket. "I represent the law and you got about ten seconds for your memory to get a whole lot better, or I'll bring you in to my immigration buddies and see if you're legal in this country or not. And believe me, little lady, legal or not, it's not an experience your want to experience. Do we understand each other?"

The lady nodded her head in understanding, but looked unsure in her actions. Derrick paused for a moment to give her time to digest what he had just told her. He was bluffing, of course, he didn't know anyone at INS, besides she was probably legal anyway. It had been his experience over the years when dealing with foreigners that the mere threat of interrogation brought to the surface stories from their own homeland, and more likely than not, they would try to avoid anything that involved getting immigration involved.

As she stood there teetering which way she would ultimately decide to go, a strong confident voice from the backroom could be heard.

"What you want to scare my girl for?" questioned the unseen voice. "And why do you seek a dead witch?"

"Dead?" Derrick repeated, obviously surprised by the new information.

"Yes, dead, she died about two years ago. It was pretty big news down here, how did you not hear about it?" the voice questioned Derrick, continuing to remain hidden.

"I've been away for a while," Derrick confessed, trying to peer through the curtain to determine who he was talking to.

"What do you want?" the voice asked, as she emerged through the bead curtain.

She was a middle-aged woman, with a bad complexion, sunken eyes, and buckteeth. Her tightly wrapped dew wrap hid her dirty, unkempt hair, which looked like something could have been living in it. But it was the smell that really blocked almost all of Derrick's thoughts. The body odor was so strong, it almost made him physically ill. Derrick had been in the presence of people who smelled worse, but they had all been dead for several days. He wondered how anyone could smell so bad and stand to be around themselves, much less others.

"I'm investigating a series of murders here in the quarter," Derrick explained, "I need information about Voodoo Rituals, do you think you can help me?"

THE MARDI GRAS MURDERS

"My name is Marie Thibodaux," the foul-smelling woman said. "Madam Thibodaux was my mother," Marie explained, staring at Derrick as though she was looking right through him. After a long silent pause, she said, "Follow me."

Marie disappeared behind the bead curtain with Derrick close behind. The back room was dark, dusty, and full of junk. The candles on the back wall were the only source of light in an otherwise darkened room.

"What the hell!" Derrick screamed as he noticed a live chicken only inches away from him. The bird was sitting on top of a stack of boxes. No cage, no nothing, just sitting on the box, fearful of nothing.

"Don't scare my bird," Marie said, as she walked to the makeshift altar against the wall. The altar consisted of various photo's of individuals, but Derrick had no way of knowing who they might be. Candles lit the surrounding area, revealing skulls with candles protruding from the top. Some were spattered with blood, and a lot of white feathers were scattered about.

"Ask your question," she said, sitting down next to a small chair beside the altar.

"There has been a series of murder in the French Quarter," Derrick began. "There was use of what I believe might be Voodoo in the last murder, but they have all been killed in the same way, I need to know what it means."

"Let me see what you got," she said, as she brushed a few feathers off her long dress.

Derrick removed his camera phone from his pocket and scanned a series of photos until he came across Liza's murder scene. Finding the photo, he handed it to Marie, who was unmoved by it's graphic nature.

"Does this scene resemble a Voodoo ritual you've ever seen?" Derrick asked, positioning himself so he could view the photo with Marie. "The cross was scratched into him with a chicken foot, and the blood was probably the victim's. There was no indication of any animals ever being on the premises," Derrick explained, trying to give her details the photo may not have offered.

"I've seen this before," Marie said, casually, "but it was back in Jamaica. Wait here," she said, handing Derrick his phone as she left the room.

Derrick felt a little uneasy being left in the room, even though he tried not to show it, leaning against one of the large boxes, he waited for Marie to return. Feeling something on his shoulder, Derrick shrugged his shoulders, not thinking too much about it. Once again, he felt pressure on his shoulder, just as he was turning to see what it was, the snake, which had put pressure on his shoulder with the main base of its body, now uncoiled and fell across his chest.

THE MARDI GRAS MURDERS

CHAPTER SIX

"Ahhhhhhh!" Derrick screamed and ran forward into the darkness, hitting a wall at full force, which sent him sprawling on the floor. Derrick, was dazed and confused as he felt the giant boa constrictor slither onto his chest. Its beady eyes looking into Derrick's.

Slowly trying not to excite the gigantic reptile anymore than was necessary, Derrick reached for his pistol, never taking his eye off the snake. Just when he had his pistol and was about to blow the snake's head off, Marie returned.

"What you think you doing with my snake!" Marie said, as she entered the room. "Good manners dictate you ask permission before playing with other people's pets." Marie said, leaning down to pick up her snake. "Come here, baby, did the mean detective scare you?" she asked, as she kissed its large head.

"Me scare her?" Derrick said, getting to his feet and securing his revolver in his holster.

After returning her snake to the box it had slid from, Marie retrieved the very old book she had walked in with.

"This book was used to exorcise demons," Marie began to explain."

The book was obviously very old, with tattered fringes as one might suspect of a book like that. But the deceptive age of the book was only part of the marketing, giving the would-be buyer the feel of purchasing something old. It was not even a first edition, Derrick keenly noted as Marie began to open the book. He was actually looking at a fourth edition released that was being sold to the general public.

"It looks like someone went to the trouble of making it look like a Voodoo ritual, but they may have gotten the idea from this book," Marie explained, opening the book to a drawing similar to that of the victims in his crime scenes.

Derrick's jaw dropped, he could not believe how close his crimes scenes were in relationship to the drawing.

With the obvious exception of furniture difference, the scene was identical to his crime scenes.

"What kind of sick ritual is this?" Derrick demanded, flipping through the pages.

"Ritual yes, sick maybe," Marie said, "I guess it depends upon your perspective. When you're cursed with a demon, you will stop at nothing to get rid of them." Marie continued, "This book demonstrates some of the lengths people throughout history have taken to purge themselves of the demons."

"Why would they remove the genitals?" Derrick asked.

"Many cultures believe when you possess a part of a man, you process the man. Like warriors who keep the shrunken heads of the men they kill, it really is nothing new, just different," Marie explained.

"How many of these books have you sold in the last three years?" Derrick questioned. "Do you have records?" he asked, hoping he might just get lucky with a receipt.

"Do we look like a bank?" Marie asked sarcastically. "This is a cash business and we've sold a bunch."

THE MARDI GRAS MURDERS

Derrick now knew someone had copied a spell out of the book. "It just couldn't be a coincidence," Derrick thought. "There were just too many similarities between the crime scenes and the photos in the book."

What troubled Derrick the most was the murderer's eye for detail; the head, hand positions and body placement were virtually identical in all the crime scene photos. It would have to be someone with an eye for detail, and this would ultimately make him all the more difficult to catch.

Dismissing the possibility of a real witch, Derrick believed the murders were very specific, yet random. They always occurred around Mardi Gras, and targeted gays. Yet, there was no obvious connection between the victims other than the fact that they were gay.

If it were someone practicing Voodoo, the killings would probably be more frequent. Individuals involved in Voodoo look upon it as a religion. Just as churchgoers would not miss church, so too the Voodoo practitioner could not go a year without another sacrifice.

"That'll be ninety nine dollars," Marie said, stretching her hand out for the money.

Reaching into his wallet for the money, Derrick returned with a hundred and handed it to Marie.

"And ten dollars tax," Marie continued, just as Derrick was returning his wallet to his pocket.

Derrick's expression sank in disbelief, but knowing he was not in a position to negotiate, he reluctantly paid her the money.

"Is there anything else I can do for you, Detective?" Marie asked, straightening out her long dress.

"I think that's it," said Derrick, "I appreciate your help."

THE MARDI GRAS MURDERS

Leaving the Voodoo Shop, Derrick merged into the crowded street.

The streets were crowded with Mardi Gras goers of every description imaginable, many in costume, some were not. It was a total conglomeration of people with one thing in common; to have a good time.

Music bleed out into the streets from the various jazz clubs. Each club was competing for as many of the tourist dollars as possible. Most of the local bars counted on a boom business that would carry them into the summer, which would be the height of tourist season.

He reflected back momentarily to the fun times he had shared in the Quarter, getting crazy with his friends. Derrick was able to hold his own and party with the best of them. But that was when he was so much younger.

Today, Derrick could not remember the last time he actually had a good time. He could still hold his liquor with the best of them, but over time, it had begun to lose its appeal. Derrick found it harder to find and maintain drinking buddies. Most men his age had settled down. Domestic tranquility was not in his cards, however, and he continued to find his comfort and pleasure in the bottle. He often thought of how much his work had cost him over the years. Work was all that existed for Derrick now, and he threw himself into it.

Looking at his watch, it was four forty-five. He did not want to be late to meet Lena. Derrick hurried as fast as the sea of people he had to transverse would allow.

Rounding a corner, Derrick came face to face with a woman dressed in a Jester outfit. She danced about as she handed out flyers, most of them were taken then later discarded. This did not matter to her as much as not accepting a flyer at all. If you, for whatever your reason may be, refused to accept her gracious offer of a

THE MARDI GRAS MURDERS

flyer, it became a personal challenge for her to get a flyer to you even if she had to force it on you. Derrick knew this and accepted the flyer right away.

For some reason not even known to Derrick, he decided to read the flyer before discarding it. He couldn't remember how many flyers he' had been handed over the years, only to be discarded without so much as a glance. Today, however, for the first time, Derrick read the flyer.

"The Decadence Parade!" the flyer read, right on Royal Street at six this evening. Paying little attention to the significance the flyer would have in the near future, Derrick shoved it in his pocket.

"Great!" Derrick thought. "Not only Bacchus is rolling tonight, but we have this Decadence Parade to boot!"

Reflecting on the earlier revelation he had about the address numbers, Derrick wondered how he would be able to dedicate enough resources to cover all the possible street locations. But he knew that Bob would never reassign resources on his hunch.

The police station was a buzz with activity, though it was Sunday, and like all police crews, overtime was the order of the day and labs were no exception. Heading downstairs to the lab, Derrick tried to quicken his step.

Steps away from the lab, Derrick once again looked at his watch. "Ten minutes late!" he thought, "I hate it when I'm late."

The police lab was located in the basement of the Police Station; "Pretty convenient," he thought, reflecting back to his Chicago lab, which was located across town.

Entering the lab, Derrick spotted a woman across the room. The lab, now dimly lit, cast an ominous scene full of various glass testing equipment ready for the

63

various uses it would be called upon. The desk was the only spot in the lab that was highly illuminated. An incandescent lamp provided light to the young attractive woman laboring at it.

"Hello," Derrick offered his usual cheerful greeting. "I'm looking for Lena."

"I'm Lena," she said, without looking up "and you must be Derrick." She glanced at her watch, "Hummm, nearly five fifteen, where has the time gone," Lena said, with a tone that Derrick picked up on immediately.

"I'm sorry," Derrick began to offer an excuse, from his mental Rolodex of excesses.

"Don't worry about it," Lena said, looking up at Derrick for the first time.

"Boy! She's a looker!" Derrick thought, then immediately glanced at her left hand. "Hummm, no ring this is good," he thought.

As Lena rose from behind the desk, handing him the lab reports he had requested, this was first opportunity to fully appreciate her slender body. He carelessly lingered his stare to a point it was obvious what he was doing.

"Detective!" Lena said, interrupting his stare. "Is there anything else?" Lena asked, as she removed her coat from behind the chair.

"Yes," Derrick said, as he returned to reality. "Have dinner with me."

"Excuse me?" Lena countered, surprised by his forwardness.

"I need to go over these reports with you," Derrick began to explain, "and besides, I owe it to you for taking care of them so soon."

"Well," Lena teetered momentarily in indecision.

"You pick the restaurant," Derrick said, as he helped her with her coat.

THE MARDI GRAS MURDERS

"Ok," she replied, surprising herself with her impulsiveness as they headed out the building.

It was early evening when they emerged from the police station. The streets were full once again, it seemed more so at night than during the day. Two blocks over, you could hear the roar of the crowds as they walked the Parade of Decadence.

"It's Sunday already," Derrick thought as he and Lena headed to a restaurant next to Farmers Market. "Two days left and it would be over for another year," Derrick thought. "He needed a break, and it would have to come pretty soon."

"We'll, Mr. Hot-shot detective from Chicago, how's your case going?" Lena asked, as they passed St. Louis Cathedral.

"I don't recall telling you I was from Chicago," Derrick said, just a little curious of how she knew. Then again, it was no secret around the station that they had brought him in, and for what.

"I know we work in the basement, but we're not all mushrooms," Lena said, with a smile and a laugh. "We hear things sometimes."

"So what do you hear?" Derrick asked, pressing Lena for more.

"Derrick Riggs," Lena continued, "Graduated from St. Mary academy in 1976, moved to Chicago in 77, married, one child, your brother is the captain of the New Orleans Police department, and you are considered the foremost criminologist of serial killers. Did I leave anything out?" she asked with a smile.

Derrick was floored at how much she knew about him. "How could she possible know so much about me?" he wondered, as they entered the open courtyard of a local restaurant just off Decatur. Derrick chose an out of the way table toward the rear.

"Hello." A waiter was at the table almost before they sat down to bring them water and a menu. "Could I start you off with something from the bar?" he asked, as he produced a pad and pencil.

"Yes, I'll have a double bourbon," Derrick stated.

"And for the lady?" the waiter inquired, waiting on Lena to place her order.

"I'll have a glass of white wine," Lena said, with a big smile.

The water left for the drinks, leaving Lena and Derrick alone to talk.

"Well, tell me Lena," Derrick asked. "How is it you know so much about me? And better yet, the fact that Bob's my brother."

Lena smiled a big smile, not saying anything immediately, as though waiting as long as she could, trying to keep Derrick in suspense, then finally she spoke.

"You don't recognize me, do you?" Lena asked, smiling wide, getting a great deal of joy out of his bewilderment.

"No," Derrick responded quickly. "Should I."

"Does the name Lena Karowski ring a bell?" Lena asked, knowing the additional clue would explain everything.

"Lena Karowski?" Derrick repeated, pausing only for a moment before recalling who she was.

"Lena Karowski from High School?" Derrick questioned triumphantly. He would have never recognized her; in High she had braces and wore thick glasses, and was a little on the chubby side. A sharp contrast to the fox that sat at the table with him now.

"But that explain everything," Derrick reasoned to himself, "if she knew me and my brother in High School."

THE MARDI GRAS MURDERS

"Well," Derrick pressed further, "I know now how you knew Bob was my brother, but how did you know about Chicago, my wife, and son?" Derrick questioned, still puzzled.

"I have a small confession to make," Lena began to explain. "I had the biggest crush on you in High School."

"Really?" Derrick said, as he smiled, flattered by the revelation.

"Whenever I'm in the Captain's office I try to ask about you. Once, I saw a picture of your son on his desk. Handsome boy," she explained, smiling before continuing again. "I guess I'm just a little nosy."

Derrick was really taken aback. He never knew Lena had the crush in High School. Not that it would have made a difference. She was a homely looking girl back then, but wow, look at her now.

"You were very accurate in your assessment, Lena except for one thing. I'm divorced now," Derrick explained.

"Really?" Lena said, in a surprised tone. "I'm sorry to hear that," Lena said, concealing her true feelings.

Seeing Derrick again just brought back a rush of emotion she had not experienced since High School. Twenty years later she still found herself attracted to Derrick.

"This is so strange," she thought, "how after so many years can emotions be revived."

"How close are you in your case?" she asked, curious about his progress.

"Not very close," Derrick explained, downing what was left of his drink and quickly ordering another. "What did the autopsy reveal?" he asked, as he reached for the envelope Lena had given him at the lab.

THE MARDI GRAS MURDERS

"Well," Lena began her narrative as Derrick looked over the report. "It seems the victim may have been hit with a stun gun, noted in the photo."

The photo showed what appeared to be two small elliptical burns about an inch and a half apart. "These are autopsy photos, I thought you just did lab work?" Derrick asked.

"We crossover a lot," Lena said with a smile, "I actually go out to the field on occasion."

"Really?" Derrick said, surprised. "The lab people in Chicago don't cross over."

"Y'all must have a bigger operating budget," Lena laughed. "Also," Lena continued, "I found an adhesive residue about the victim's mouth, which we see a lot of in victims that have been bound and gagged."

"Anything else?" Derrick asked, as he continued to glance over her report.

"Yes, swelling of tissue around the lacerations would indicate that he was alive through most of the ordeal. Not a whole lot to go on, is it?" Lena concluded, seeing the anxiety in Derrick's face.

"No it's not," Derrick agreed, putting the folder away.

For the rest of the evening, Derrick and Lena tried to put behind them the ugliness of their business. They spent the rest of the evening catching up on where the last twenty years had gone.

CHAPTER SEVEN

The Parade of Decadence was just getting started. To the casual onlooker, he looked like any other tourist that populated the streets to see this gay and lesbian parade. He was no tourist though, and his motivation was not to have a good time, not yet. He had spent days stalking his prey, he now knew just when the best time would be to take down his next victim.

He spotted him from a distance, through fifty other homosexuals, frolicking in a parade entitled the Dorothy March. The mark had a feature, which made him stand out. The large nose prominent on his narrow face made him easy to spot at seventy yards.

He was proceeding along the parade route with about fifty other men all dressed like Judy Garland, in the Wizard of Oz. How could he possible know he only had a few hours left to live?

The merriment would continue on well into the night, but his Dorothy would shut it down early that night. He watched as his soon to-be victim turned down Decatur St., acting as though he did not have a care in the world. Singing as he walked, then every so often, breaking out in a quick dance step. There was no way he could possibly know that he was being watched. His every move measured and calculated, most were predictable.

In the shadows, only thirty yards behind him was another dance closing in on him, it was the dance of death. As the Dorothy turned the corner and headed down a narrow alley, he was close behind. The alley opened into a beautiful courtyard, surrounded by a series of low-rent apartments, each facing the courtyard.

Waiting only long enough for his light to come on inside his apartment, he prepared to pounce on his unsuspecting prey. There was no other light in the surrounding apartments that would indicate anyone else was home. They were all probably still out celebrating. Not that it would matter, he had waited too long for this moment. "One swift kick to the door and I'm in!" he thought, playing the scenario in his mind.

The moment had arrived, his commitment was total. Kicking in the door, he rushed to find his startled prey. Grabbing his prey, he threw him hard on the floor. Stunned and scared, the man lay motionless staring at his assailant as though in shock. Gagging and bounding him only took a few seconds, since he did not offer any resistance. He had his stun gun handy just in case, but the man proved to be so timid, he did not need it.

His Dorothy now lay bound and gagged on the floor.

Now he would be able to take his time, and do what he had come for.

Derrick was going to be awoken from his deep slumber in the same manner he had been the previous morning.

CHAPTER EIGHT

Bang! Bang! Bang! The door vibrated with each pounding of its unknown assailant.

Dragging himself out of bed, Derrick threw open the door. "What!" he yelled, as the door flew open, coming face to face with Mark, holding a cup of coffee.

"Good morning, Detective," Mark said, handing Derrick the coffee as he tried to follow Derrick back in the room.

"The captain sent me to get you," Mark explained.

Derrick blocked the door momentarily, looking over his shoulder; Lena was heading for the bathroom. After she was safely hidden out of sight, Derrick allowed Mark to enter.

As Mark entered the room, one of the first things he noticed was the dress laid across a chair, and the undergarments on the floor.

"Can I use your restroom?" Mark asked, dying to know whom Derrick had hidden in the bathroom.

"NO!" Derrick responded immediately, he knew what Mark was up to. "You're not going to be here that long."

"Are you going to continue to be a hard ass," Mark asked, "or are we going to be able to work together?"

Derrick sidestepped the question, "What's up, Mark?"

THE MARDI GRAS MURDERS

"We have another one," Mark began, "found this morning, same MO."

"Give me a minute," Derrick said, trying to shake the cobwebs from his head.

Anxious to get Mark out of the room as soon as possible, Derrick slipped on his slacks and put on a fresh shirt, then he and Mark was out the door.

With Mark leading the way, Derrick followed. Within what seemed only a few minutes, they were turning onto Decatur.

Derrick stopped in his tracks.

"Mark?" Derrick asked. "What street did the murder occur on?"

"Decatur," Mark said, "why?"

Derrick stared up at the street sign, "Rue Decatur." He could not help but remember the name of the parade that rolled last night, "Decadence!" This reinforced his suspicions, but the streets were long and the houses many. If he was going to stand a chance at solving this case he would have to somehow narrow down the address.

"Just asking," Derrick said, unwilling to share with Mark his suspicions.

Passing Jackson Square, Derrick could not help but recall he had been right here the very night the murder had taken place. Turning into a small alley, Mark led Derrick to the crime scene.

Entering the crime scene, the first thing Derrick noticed was the familiarity. Between the last scene he had investigated, and his review of the photos from the previous murders, it was a scene he had become way too familiar with.

"Is there anything different than the last one?" Derrick asked, finding the detective in charge.

THE MARDI GRAS MURDERS

"No," he said, "we went over the area, but nothing different. It's as though someone took a photo and transposed it over our crime scene."

Derrick's sharp eye spotted something by the post of the bed, but did not immediately rush to it. If there was one thing he learned in his career, it was not to trust anybody. Derrick had also been a firm believer in the old adage that rules were never broken, but may be bent until they are unrecognizable.

As Derrick looked upon the scene in the bedroom, the detective had only suggested a general similarity. He did not see as Derrick did, the little things about it that made it identical. The hand position down, the curvature of the fingers, to the exact feet position. The cuts in his chest and placement of the stab wound also so close they could only be differentiated with a millimeter gauge.

As the detective momentarily left the room to talk to Mark, Derrick seized the opportunity to retrieve the clue he had spotted next to the bedpost.

A silver piece of a charm lay behind the bedpost.

"I've seen this before," he thought, "in fact, it was on a charm on one of the first people I met here."

"VOODOO!" Derrick's mind screamed out the connection.

Removing a plastic envelope from his pocket, Derrick placed it in the envelope, and secured it back in his pocket just as the detective reentered the room.

"You found something?" he asked.

"Just tying my shoe," Derrick replied, not willing to share his new information with anyone.

Derrick left the room just as Lena was arriving with two rather stout gentlemen pulling a gurney. Unlike Derrick, she had obviously showered and gotten herself together better than Derrick.

THE MARDI GRAS MURDERS

Lena smiled wide upon seeing Derrick; there was a definite attraction on her part to Derrick, if last night had not removed any doubt. Derrick also felt something, both emotionally and physically. It was something he was going to pursue. Derrick knew, opportunities only occasionally presented themselves. Derrick had no intention of letting this opportunity slip away from him.

"We'll, Detective," Lena whispered, smiling wide. "We meet again, I told you I came to the field now and then."

"So you did," Derrick smiled.

Derrick kept smiling, he felt like a school kid again. He couldn't remember ever feeling the way he felt with Lena before, not even with his wife. Last night was the most fantastic night he had spent in a long time. He found himself attracted to Lena, it was more than just wanting to get in her pants, although that was what ended up happening. They seemed to be more; he was able to talk to Lena like he had not been unable to talk to anyone before. Maybe it was the fact that they both saw the darkest side of humanity, and some how was able to understand the pain they both often felt. Whatever it was, Derrick was going to make it a point to pursue every opportunity with Lena that presented itself.

"Lena, I, ah, was ah," Derrick stumbled over his words like a kid asking for his first date. Seeing his nervousness and awkwardness, Lena decided to rescue Derrick from himself.

"Derrick," Lena interrupted him, "you want to get together tonight?"

"You read my mind," Derrick said, finally finding his voice. "Were would you like to go?"

THE MARDI GRAS MURDERS

"My place," Lena explained, "I'll cook you dinner, here's my card, I wrote the directions on the back. Say about seven?"

"It's a date," Derrick said, just as the gurney rolled by with the body of the apartment's occupant.

Derrick was surprised to see how much blood the white sheet covering the body had absorbed. Derrick thought that every drop of blood had been drained from the body, or dried on the wounds.

As the stretcher rolled by, both Lena and Derrick were brought back to the reality of the moment.

"Later," Lena said, turning to Derrick, then following the gurney on its way to the morgue.

"You've met our coroner before?" Mark asked as he walked up to Derrick, seeing how they had looked at each other.

"Yes," Derrick replied, as he too left the building, not elaborating further.

Derrick knew just what Mark was doing. He was on a fishing expedition trying to find out all he could about himself and Lena. Derrick had known plenty of guys like this, they were the biggest gossiper at the water cooler, many times causing a great deal of pain to those around them. If one thing was for sure, he didn't want to create any problems for Lena.

"Where did you meet her?" Mark continued to question, hoping to get just a little more out of Derrick.

Derrick did not know it, but Mark had a little history with Lena. He had tried for the longest time to get her to go out with him, but she would not give him the time of day.

Turning to Mark, Derrick said, "Mark, let me explain this one more time, my personal life is just that: personal. I thought I made that clear at the Pink Flamingo."

Positioning himself right in front of Mark, making

sure he had eye contact, like you would do a small child, he continued, "Are you listening to me, Mark?" Derrick asked, waiting for a response.

"I'm listening," Mark said, getting agitated once again by what he knew was coming.

"You're here because the captain says you got to be here. I don't ask you a million questions, so don't ask me. You got to get a better grip on this temporary working relationship."

"You know," Mark said, "You're a real prick!" I've tried twice, because the captain gave me this assignment."

Mark was turning red, he was so mad it looked as though he could have taken a swing at Derrick at any moment. Derrick saw his fist clench. Knowing he had pushed him about as far as he could to the edge, now it was time to make him back down. Moving to within less than an inch from Mark's face, he spoke. "It's your move," Derrick offered, knowing there was a fifty-fifty chance Mark would swing on him.

"Nothing between us but air and opportunity," Derrick offered again, staring Mark hard in the eyes.

Mark was the first to blink, and as before, he stormed off down the street. As Derrick began his trek back to police headquarters, bands and the sounds of screaming crowds could be heard in distance. Another small impromptu parade had formed and had chosen Jackson Square as their parade route.

As Derrick headed out the apartment and through the door leading to the street. The apartment number was prominently displayed, "twenty-three." Derrick made another mental note of the number, he knew it might come in handy latter.

Sliding through the crowd, Derrick headed back to the station. Retrieving the charm he had taken from the scene, he knew he was going to have to get to know Voodoo Jones a little better.

He remembered seeing the charm on Voodoo. "That would make so much sense," Derrick thought. "Each time they had investigated recently, and in the past, the crime scene had been all but void of any practical evidence."

He had investigated plenty of crime scenes in the past, and regardless of how careful the killer thought he was, he always left clues of some kind. But if it was Voodoo, who better to remove evidence from a scene than a policeman. After all, he knows just what to look for and where.

Arriving at the police station, Derrick took the steps two at a time, anxious to see Voodoo. The station was crowded, large events and huge crowds brought together everything from pickpockets to brawls.

Bloody individuals, who had tried to make the streets their personal boxing ring, awaited processing. A besieged police force was trying to cope the best they knew how.

Going directly to his brother's office, he barged in, not slowing down to knock.

"Bob!" Derrick began, excitement evident in his voice. "What can you tell me about Voodoo?"

Bob was already standing, he had jumped to his feet when Derrick barged in. Pointing his finger in Derrick's face first, then to the chair.

"Voodoo your ass in that chair!" Bob demanded.

"But Bob!" Derrick tried to explain.

"It's Captain to you! Who the hell do you think you are, barging into my office like that! I don't care if you're my brother or not, when you're down here, you will conduct yourself in a professional manner, do I make myself clear?" Bob paused, waiting for a sign from Derrick that he understood. He could feel how red his face was, and he felt his heart pound heavily in his chest. He knew this amount of anxiety was not good for him, but he was going to drive his point home to Derrick if it killed him.

Derrick shook his head in understanding, he felt scared, not from the ass chewing Bob had just administered to him. He had been chewed out by far better than Bob. What scared Derrick most was the way Bob looked. He knew his brother did not take very good care of himself and was a prime candidate for a heart attack. Knowing he could not live with himself if that happened, he attempted to calm Bob down.

"Calm down, Captain, please!" Derrick pleaded. "I'm sorry for everything, just calm down."

Bob began to calm down a little. Throwing himself down in his chair, he pulled his hand across his graying hair.

"What's the hell's wrong with you, Derrick?" Bob began. "You can't go around talking to my detectives any way you want!"

Realizing only now why Bob had been so upset, apparently, Mark had reported him to Bob over their little tiff.

"Bob, it wasn't as bad as you heard," Derrick tried to explain his version of the events, but Bob wasn't having any of it.

"I don't give a shit what happened!" Bob said, not allowing Derrick to continue. "But I tell you what's gonna happen; you gonna apologize to Mark, and we're all gonna put this behind us. I don't know how you act up there in Chicago, but down here in Na Awlins, you gonna have some manners."

Bob picked up the phone and quickly punched out a series of numbers. When he had punched the last number, the party must have been waiting. Almost instantaneously when he pushed the last number, the party being called must have picked up.

"Get in here!" Bob ordered, then slammed down the receiver. In short order, Mark was tapping on Bob's door.

"Get in here and close the door!" Bob ordered, as Mark complied.

"You two get this straight, because this is the only time I'm going to say it!" Bob's voice was firm, no nonsense. "Mark, Derrick is here because he is the best at what he does, you are to cooperate with him in anyway possible, got it?"

Mark nodded his head in understanding, though his facial expression gave a much different message. He was still furious at the way Derrick had treated him, and given his choice, he would have preferred not to work with Derrick at all. In fact, that had been his intent when he told the captain about their exchange, hoping the personality clash would have been enough for the captain to replace him. Apparently it wasn't.

"And you!" the captain continued, "you were requested on this case by me, and I can un-request you. Mark is your sponsor, while you're here, to make sure you don't do nothing stupid. You don't have a choice in this, is that clear?"

"Absolutely," Derrick said, "I will make every effort to get along with my partner, thank you for bring to my attention my short comings. I will try to meet the expectation that you and the department have for me."

Bob looked at Derrick hard, knowing he was just telling him what he wanted to hear. He didn't really care though, as long as he didn't get any more complaints about him.

"Is that all, captain?" Derrick asked.

"Both of you, get out of here," Bob instructed the two detectives.

THE MARDI GRAS MURDERS

Leaving the office with Derrick, Mark turned to Derrick as they walked down the hall.

"Listen, I think we got off to a bad start," Mark began. "Let's start over," Mark offered, extending his hand to Derrick.

Whatever Derrick had thought of Mark before, it had only been magnified by his whining to the captain. Derrick didn't like Mark, he couldn't put his finger on it, but something was not right. He sensed something though, he wasn't sure what. Derrick knew after the ass chewing they both received that Mark would not be going back to the captain anytime soon, so there was no real reason for him to reconcile their differences. He had always been a loner, and worked best that way. By pissing off Mark, he would surely go out of his way and let him do his job. So, as Mark held his outstretched hand out toward him.

Derrick simply smiled in that broad smile of his, and said, "Blow me!" And walked away.

Mark was even more furious than before, but unlike before when he went to the Captain, Mark was not going back; he would simply investigate the best he could and the hell with Derrick. This was the third time he had tried to find common ground. There would not be a fourth. He didn't care if Derrick heard about the next murder or not.

CHAPTER NINE

Derrick headed to Voodoo's desk to see if he was in. When he reached the desk, he wasn't there, but what he did find was far more interesting. To his surprise, there on the desk was some of his case files on the Mardi Gras murders. This definitely raised a flag for Derrick, because Voodoo had his personal notes attached to the files. Notes that indicated what direction he was going in, what he was looking for. Questions he often posed to himself on elements of the crime that did not make sense. If you were the murderer, this information would prove invaluable to help cover your tracks. At this point, Derrick began to suspect Voodoo even more than before.

Heading to the sergeant's desk, Derrick was going ascertain exactly where Voodoo was. Behind the sergeant's desk was a middle-aged gray-haired man with a round belly.

"Excuse me," said Derrick, getting the desk sergeant's attention.

"Yes," the gruff police officer replied.

"Do you know where I can find Voodoo?" Derrick asked.

"He's out," the Sergeant reported, "called in sick. Too much Mardi Gras I guess."

"Another piece to the puzzle," Derrick thought, "he had the time to stalk his victims before killing them."

"Do you have an address on him?" Derrick asked.

"You that detective from up north?" the sergeant asked, to verify his identify before releasing any information.

"Yes, my name is Derrick Riggs from Chicago," he explained.

"Yea. Ok, the captain told us to help you if you asked, here you go," the sergeant said, handing him a piece of paper he had scribbled the address on.

"What you want with Voodoo?" the sergeant asked, obviously curious by nature.

"I just want his insight on the case I'm working, I understand he worked on it," Derrick said, concealing his true motivation.

"That's an understatement," the sergeant said, "he was obsessed with it. Worked on the case all the time, night and day."

Derrick was puzzled now; his first lead and it may turn out to be an obsessive detective. "Or," Derrick surmised, it could have been a detective working diligently to cover his tracks. Whatever it turned out to be, one thing was sure. It was his only lead, he had to either clear Voodoo or find evidence to convict him.

Derrick left the station and headed back to his hotel, the Holiday Inn in the French Quarter. It was a nice hotel located just off Canal St, the hotel was situated right at the beginning of the French Quarter. Entering the lobby, Derrick weaved his way in and out of people looking for that impossible to find room, most having been booked three years in advance.

Stopping off briefly at his room just long enough to retrieve the book he had bought from the Voodoo shop, Derrick headed for his car. Taking the lobby elevator to the third floor garage parking lot, he looked for his rental car, not having used it for some time, he had forgotten precisely where he had parked it in the crowded parking lot. Locating his car, he tossed his Voodoo book on the passenger seat then headed out, destination: Voodoo's house.

Progress was slow as he turned onto Canal St. Moving at a snail's pace, the mass of party goers spilling over from the boulevards and sidewalks onto the streets, which made speed impossible.

Eventually, Derrick was able to leave the downtown area, and head into an area of New Orleans far less crowded. It was not long before he found himself in un-chartered territory, and lost. With no other option, he broke down and consulted a map. The map indicated he was in close proximity to Voodoo's house.

Arriving at the address he parked a safe distance from Voodoo's house to observe him. Not wanting to alert him, Derrick knew he would have to keep a safe distance. Voodoo's car was in the drive and it didn't seem like he was ready to leave anytime soon.

Derrick looked at his watch; it was three in the afternoon. He would watch Voodoo's house for a few hours more, then he had to leave for Lena's house. His intent was not to follow Voodoo, he'd see him coming a mile away. What Derrick needed to do was to break into his house and look for anything that would tie him into the killings. This would, of course, require Voodoo to leave. Hours passed and with no opportunity presenting itself, Derrick headed for Lena's house.

Lena lived in an upscale apartment building of St Charles Street, this proved convenient for her to get to and from work without fighting traffic jams. She simply hopped on the streetcar and it brought her right up to Canal Street, only one block from the police station.

THE MARDI GRAS MURDERS

While the location proved convenient for Lena, the parking situation was a different story. Derrick spent some time circling the block looking for an up to now, elusive parking space. Finally Derrick was able to locate a parking spot right off St Charles itself. Retrieving his book, he hurried to meet Lena.

Crossing the threshold of the front door of the lobby, Derrick was stopped by the doorman.

"May I help you, sir?" the middle-aged man asked, as he positioned himself between Derrick and the elevator.

"Yes," Derrick explained, "I'm here to see Ms. Lena Karowski."

"Very well, sir, but I'll have to announce you first," the doorman answered very politely. "If you would," he continued, gesturing to a phone on the wall indicating he wanted Derrick to follow him. After quickly punching in a series of numbers, the doorman apparently reached Lena's apartment

"Ms. Karowski," the doorman began. "I have a gentleman," the doorman paused, only now realizing he had not gotten Derrick's name. Covering the receiver with one hand, he asked, "What's your name, sir?"

"Derrick Riggs," Derrick answered.

"Derrick Riggs," the doorman repeated into the receiver. "Very well, I'll send him right up." Returning the receiver to the wall, he turned to Derrick.

"She's expecting you sir," said the doorman, as he called the elevator. "She's in room four thirty-two."

Taking the elevator to the fourth floor, Derrick stood at Lena's door and knocked. It was opened immediately, as though she had been on the other side waiting for him.

"Hello, Derrick," Lena greeted Derrick with a big smile, and a quick kiss. "Come on in."

THE MARDI GRAS MURDERS

"What's that?" Lena asked, referring to Derrick's Voodoo book.

"Oh, something I wanted to show you, but we'll look at it later," Derrick said, as he entered the apartment.

"Ok," Lena agreed, heading back to the kitchen, "Make yourself at home, dinner's almost ready."

Derrick looked around her nicely decorated apartment. "Very nice," Derrick thought.

"Make yourself a drink if you want," Lena said, peering around the corner.

Derrick took her up on her offer and focused in on the scotch at the bar. Out of Lena's sight, he quickly downed two shots, then finally poured one on ice.

"Would you like one, Lena?" Derrick asked.

"No thanks, I have some wine in the fridge. How was your day?" she asked, looking out over the counter that separated the living room from the kitchen. "Any new leads?"

"Yes, I think I do." Derrick began to explain his latest revelation to Lena. "I'm starting to believe that the murderer has a great deal of knowledge about the police procedures, and could possibly be a cop."

Lena came out of the kitchen, visibly shocked by Derrick's accusation. "You've seen the way the bodies were butchered, do you really think one of our people could be doing this?"

"I do," Derrick, said, "I have a suspect, but I'm not sure."

"Who is it?" Lena asked, trying to find out who in a department she knew so well could be capable of this.

"You know I can't accuse anyone without hard evidence, and he's only a suspect," Derrick cautioned Lena.

Lena nodded her head in understanding.

"But what can you tell me about Voodoo Jones?"

THE MARDI GRAS MURDERS

"You suspect Voodoo?" Lena questioned, pausing momentarily to compose herself.

"Yes, I do, now what can you tell me about him?" Derrick pushed Lena for information.

Lena sat on the couch, Derrick followed, sitting next to her.

"Well," Lena began, "I had heard he did dabble in Voodoo practices. I don't know how much of that is true or not."

"Do you remember the cases he was involved with in regard to these murders?" Derrick asked.

"Well, the news of these murders were big news around her, everybody knew Voodoo was in charge of the investigation before you came," Lena explained, surprised that Derrick did not know this.

"Really," Derrick responded in surprise. "I guess that explains even more. It's no wonder none of the cases were solved if he was the one doing the killing."

"You know the killings were part of some sort of Voodoo ritual," Derrick informed Lena. "The precise position of the bodies, and the method of killing, look at this." Derrick took the book he had bought from the Voodoo shop and opened it to the photo he had seen earlier.

Lena was aghast, "It's identical!" Lena said, staring at the photo then flipping a few pictures forward and back before beginning to read the text. "Some sort of ritual, it says here a ritual to keep demons at bay."

"What's your next move?" Lena asked, curious to know where he would begin.

"Well, I think he has a pattern, he kills every other night, and the name of the street he kills on matches the name of the parade that rolls that day," Derrick explained. "So if I'm right, Rex is rolling Tuesday, and he'll strike somewhere on Royal street."

"Royal is a big street," Lena said.

THE MARDI GRAS MURDERS

"I know, there's, my dilemma," Derrick explained, "but enough about work."

He took Lena's wine glass and set it on the table next to his. He softly cupped her face in his hands, pulling her lips to his. Looking deep into her eyes, moving closer, he closed his eyes as their lips met and slowly parted, allowing him to explore her tongue with his. He warmed quickly to the heat of their passions, as did she, embracing him with her arms as tightly as her strength would allow.

She pushed Derrick away and he reluctantly complied, putting on hold only momentarily the passion that had surfaced within her.

"Tell me more about the case," she said.

"Forget about the case," Derrick said, as he leaned her back on the couch, once again renewing the heat that had set his passion on fire. As Derrick kissed Lena, he could feel her getting just as hot as he was. He wanted her so bad, he was determined to go for it. He slid his hand under her shirt blouse and rubbed her breast thought her bra. She responded by her kiss growing more passionate.

Derrick would not waste any more time on the couch, for he wanted to take Lena on the bed, in a proper manner. Picking Lena up from the couch, he carried her into her bedroom, where his passion would only be extinguished after an entire night of making love.

THE MARDI GRAS MURDERS

CHAPTER TEN

Derrick and Lena were awakened the next morning by Lena's beeper. Quickly calling her office, she got unwelcome information.

"There's been another homicide," Lena told Derrick. "It another one of your murders."

"What!" Derrick said, shocked. "The pattern, it should have been tomorrow," he said. "Damn, I should have kept Voodoo under surveillance!"

"Derrick," Lena said, pausing for a moment. "The body they found was Voodoo."

"What! Can't be!" Completely perplexed at this point, Derrick found himself speechless.

Derrick threw on his clothes and was out the door. "Voodoo!" Derrick thought, heading back to the Quarter. "How could that be?" he wondered, "My lead suspect killed."

Arriving on Royal Street, the exact location was easy to find because of all the police cars. Since it was one of their own, the police had come out in force. Checking in with the perimeter detective, Derrick headed to the apartment. Walking through the door, Derrick noticed the number. Forty-eight was displayed on the door. He turned back to the policeman out front.

"Do you know how many floats they have for the Rex parade today?" Derrick asked, not really sure if the officer would know or not.

"Forty-eight," he said immediately.

THE MARDI GRAS MURDERS

"Are you sure?" Derrick questioned.

"Yep!" Gotta work the parade route today, that's one of the first things we find out, how many floats they have," the officer explained, "Gives us an idea when the darn thing will be over."

"Did you work the Decadence parade?" Derrick asked.

"Yes, I work all of them," the officer explained.

"Do you remember how many floats?" Derrick's started getting excited, as he anticipated the officer's response.

"Twenty-three," the officer said.

"Thank you," Derrick said, then headed toward the crime scene. "That's it!" Derrick screamed inside his thoughts, "The parades indicate the street, and the number the address!"

Although it was the rearmost section of the Quarter, an area that had historically become somewhat rundown, this complex was not; it was well kept, and clean. Entering the well-manicured courtyard, Derrick spotted Voodoo's body on the ground just outside the apartment of the next victim. He had been stabbed in the chest, but no other visual marks were on him.

"With his gun still in his holster," Derrick reasoned, "he was caught by surprise, or. ...someone he knew."

While the photographer continued to take photos, he interrupted him for a moment.

"You mind if I check his pockets?" Derrick asked the photographer as he stopped snapping photos.

"No, go ahead, I'll wait."

Reaching into Voodoo's trouser pocket, Derrick searched for the key chain he had once seen him with. Finding the key chain key, he removed it from his pocket.

THE MARDI GRAS MURDERS

To Derrick's surprise the charm was still intact, though it was identical to the piece he had found at one of the murders.

"Voodoo must have figured it out!" Derrick thought, "I know he was still working the case, the desk sergeant said he was obsessed with it. He must have surprised the murderer, so he moved up his time schedule."

Returning the key chain back to Voodoo's pocket, Derrick noticed the activity inside of one of the apartments. As he entered, he saw Mark already on location. Mark ignored him as he entered the bedroom where the second victim had been found.

Unlike the other victims, he had been bound with duct tape with his chest carved up and his genitals removed, possibly being interrupted by Voodoo before he could position the body like the previous murders. Derrick watched as the two coroners struggled with the duct tape, feeling their pocket for what Derrick thought was a knife.

"One of you guys have knife?" one of them asked.

"Here you go," Mark stepped up, offering a small pen knife, dangling from the knife was a small charm identical to that of Voodoo's, with one exception. *A PIECE HAD BEEN BROKEN OFF!*

Socked but trying not to show it, Derrick stepped closer as the coroner cut the duct tape. He was trying to get a better look at the fob.

As he peered at the dangling fob, it was very apparent that it matched the piece he found at one of the previous murders. Derrick remembered going to the scene with Mark, but Mark did not enter the room until after he found the piece. "So the only way that piece of the fob could have got at the crime scene," Derrick reasoned, *"Mark was the killer!"*

THE MARDI GRAS MURDERS

Derrick now had his killer, but he knew the fob just gave him a lead; the real evidence would have to come from somewhere else. As the crime scene was beginning to be wrapped up and the body removed, Derrick could not help but notice Mark, and Mark noticed him watching. He stared back hard, wondering what Derrick had on his mind.

"Is there a problem, Detective?" Mark asked, "you look like you got a bug up your ass."

Derrick just smiled; he knew Mark had no idea what he had just realized and how close he was to locking him up.

"You got any idea when you gonna solve this case?" Mark asked sarcastically.

"Soon," Derrick smiled once again, agitating Mark further.

"Very soon." He then went outside where Lena had just arrived.

Walking up to her, he took her by the arm and led her out of the courtyard to his car.

"I've just got a break in the case!" Derrick told her.

"That's great," Lena said, expressing her excitement.

"I need your help again though."

"Sure anything," Lena agreed.

"I need to get Mark's address," Derrick explained, knowing that the fact he now suspected Mark would raise a flag for her, because just hours earlier he had suspected Voodoo, who was now dead.

"Mark? Why?" Lena questioned, "You gonna accuse everybody in the department now?"

"Lena, I know how it sounds, but I'm asking you to believe me." Derrick pleaded his case. "I think he's the killer, and he's the one that killed Voodoo. He never quit working on the case, he was obsessed with it. He probably figured out where the next murder was going to take place. Saw Mark casing the place, he probably never suspected Mark and let him get too close. This is what got him killed."

"I know you have access to the department's computer," Derrick stated, "I need his address."

Lena reluctantly agreed and drove with Derrick to the police station, where she accessed Mark's information.

"Here it is," Lena said, as she started to hand Derrick the address. Just as Derrick was reaching for the address, she pulled it back away from him.

"You're not going without me!" she said, waiting for Derrick to agree.

"Ok, you can be a lookout; if you see him coming, you can warn me."

"I can do that," Lena agreed to her part.

Derrick and Lena headed to Mark's apartment. It was in the older part of the city and kind of run down, many of the houses had bars on the window. Always a good indicator of a criminal element present.

"That's it!" Lena said, as she pointed to Mark's house, seeing the number on the mailbox first.

Parking his car a short distance away, Derrick scanned the surrounding area. He did not see anyone outside, no delivery personnel or anyone else whose suspicion would be raised when he went to the house.

Pulling his cell phone from his pocket he called, Mark's home number. He wasn't sure if Mark lived alone or not. The last thing he wanted to do was walk in on Mark's roommate if he had one.

"No answer," Derrick told Lena. "You got my number, if you see anyone coming, call me."

"Got it!" Lena said.

Returning his phone back to his pocket, Derrick never noticed his battery was fading.

THE MARDI GRAS MURDERS

Crossing the street, Derrick once again scanned the area. Going to the back of the house where he would not be detected, he positioned himself by the rear door and went to work. Removing a lock pick kit from his pocket, he inserted it in the lock and began manipulating the tumblers, which opened relatively easy on the well worn lock.

Entering the house, he began a methodical search of the house, room by room, without revealing a single clue.

Finally coming to the bedroom, Derrick opened an amour, stepping back in surprise and disgust at what he saw.

CHAPTER ELEVEN

There, neatly arranged jars were placed on the shelves of the amour. Jars containing what appeared to be testicles. Each jar had a name neatly labeled on it.

Derrick immediately recognized the names: *they were all victims of the Mardi Gras murders!*

Just then, Derrick heard the front door open. Reaching for his pocket, he pulled his phone out; the battery was low and flashing.

"Derrick?" he heard, a familiar voice call. *"It was Mark!"*

"I know you're in here," Mark announced.

Derrick pulled his revolver and pointed it toward the bedroom door, ready for the showdown that was about to happen. Derrick heard Mark getting closer, he would be waiting.

Pointing his nine-millimeter to the door opening, Derrick's finger began to tighten on the trigger.

Just as he was about to pull the trigger, *Lena appeared in the doorway!* Mark was using her as a shield. Derrick pulled back his revolver, aiming it to the ceiling.

"Now, you be a good detective and throw down your gun," Mark instructed, "before Ms. Lena gets a bullet in her pretty head."

Lena was scared, really scared. She sobbed as quietly as she could, trying to compose herself as much as possible, given the situation she found herself in.

THE MARDI GRAS MURDERS

"It'll be all right, Lena," Derrick said, trying to reassure her. But he knew, as did she, their situation was grave.

Complying with Mark's orders, he tossed his gun to the floor.

"Why Mark?" Derrick asked. "You killed all those people."

"All fags!" he shouted, pushing Lena toward Derrick as he picked up his pistol.

"How about Voodoo?" Derrick questioned. "Was he a fag?"

"Voodoo had me figured out. Smart man he was. He figured out the location of the next killing. When he saw me there scoping out the place, he just assumed I had figured it out too, after all, I was assigned to the case. He never saw it coming, I slipped the knife right into his heart," Mark explained, without emotion, without regret.

"Of course, I had to move my timetable up a bit, and kill the old fag a little earlier than I had planned," Mark continued to explain.

"Why?" Derrick asked again.

"Why? You haven't a clue what the hell I've been though!" Mark yelled.

"Tell me, Mark," Derrick said, "I'm all ears. Why homosexuals?"

"It was three years ago during Mardi Gras," Mark began to explain. "I was drunk, minding my own business having a good time. Two queers dragged me into an ally and raped me." The pain in Mark's face could be seen as he began to relive the experience. "I was so ashamed! I'm a cop!, and I couldn't defend myself!" Mark screamed, tears starting to swell up in his eyes. "I went through the whole year, it was always on my mind, like a cancer it ate at me. Consuming me from the inside out."

THE MARDI GRAS MURDERS

"My salvation came when I was in the Voodoo shop." Mark picked up a book from a nearby shelf. "I found this book, it showed me how to keep my demons at bay!" Mark explained.

"It worked! After killing the first homo, I was able to function again, until the next year. Then the sacrifice must be made again."

"I guess you're a little better than I gave you credit for. How did you know it was me?" Mark asked, curious as to how Derrick discovered it was him.

Derrick reached into his pocket.

"Easy!" Mark cautioned, as Derrick slowly removed the portion of the key fob from his pocket.

"I found this at one of the murder scenes. I remember seeing Voodoo with one like it. When I saw his intact, I thought I was at another dead end. Until you handed the orderly your knife with the broken fob. Derrick explained.

"I wondered where the other piece went," Mark said, with a smile.

"What now?" Derrick asked. "It's over."

"Over!" Mark screamed, "Not by a long shot! We're going to go for a ride." Mark motioned for Derrick to leave the room.

As Lena began to follow Derrick out, Mark grabbed her. "I want you to stay close to me," Mark said, "just in case your boyfriend here wants to try anything."

They got in Derrick's car, Mark got in the back seat with Lena.

"Head down 90 to Fort Pike!" he ordered.

Derrick knew the place; as a boy, he and his brother had spent a lot of time there. It was an old Civil War fort build in the early 1800s.

"So how you gonna get away with this?" Derrick asked Mark, trying to keep his mind engaged.

THE MARDI GRAS MURDERS

"People show up dead all the time, you're just gonna be another statistic," he explained bluntly.

The drive toward Fort Pike did not take long. Soon they were at the entrance to the park. It was closed.

"Let's go!" Mark ordered as Derrick parked the car.

He led his two captives toward the massive door leading to the inner Fort.

From the air, the Fort took on the appearance of a baseball field arched in the rear and coming together at a ninety-degree point.

Mark tossed Derrick a key to the door.

"How did you get a key for here?" Derrick questioned, as he began to unlock the massive lock that secured the door.

"I know the guy who runs the place," Mark answered, "I use to come here on the weekends to think."

The massive wooden doors were secured by a chain wrapped through two pad eyes. Derrick unlocked the lock and began to unwrap the chain from the steel loops. As he unwrapped the chain, he wrapped it around his hand.

"A little diversion and I could brain him with this chain!" Derrick thought. He was not going to be murdered easily.

Derrick pulled open the heavy door, still holding the chain in his left hand.

"Get in there!" Mark ordered, pushing Derrick toward the door.

With a swooping motion, Derrick swung the chain. It stuck Mark hard across the face, sending him backward over the handrail and into the moat of the fort. Derrick turned to grab Lena's hand. He started to make a run across the bridge back to the car.

THE MARDI GRAS MURDERS

"BANG! BANG!" Two shots rang out, discouraging their departure. Apparently, Mark had been able to come out the water with gun in hand and ready to guard the bridge.

Derrick retreated with Lena to the concave protection of the fort walls. Inside, they ran down a long corridor, the doors opened up onto a large room, some with portholes like windows, which once accommodated cannon barrels.

Another loud crack of gunfire echoed loudly off the walls, as though it had been fired in a tunnel. The two hundred year old brick shattered into pieces as the bullet penetrated it, not far from Derrick's head. Turning the corner now, Derrick ran down the corridor until it suddenly ended. The fort dead-ended!

They were trapped! Derrick and Lena found themselves in a large room, which was in the process of being restored.

A small earthen recess existed around the room, which was in the process of being restored. Various assorted hand tools were spewed about, probably left by the workers who had planned to return. Shovels, pick axes, wheelbarrows, ect. All possible weapons, but no match for a gun.

Derrick realized that this was intended to be his and Lena's final resting place. Derrick went to the partially constructed wall and climbed over it.

After firing the two rounds at Derrick, Mark knew he had them now. The fort had only one entrance and one exit, he was now positioned in front of it. If Derrick was coming out, it was though him.

Dragging himself up the embankment of the moat, Mark ran to the front door of the fort. He peered around the corner, not wanting to be surprised again.

THE MARDI GRAS MURDERS

Turning the corner, he could see Derrick and Lena at the far wall, he fired, but missed.

"They're trapped now!" Mark thought, knowing the path they had taken led to a dead end. He ran forward and down the path that Lena and Derrick had taken.

As Mark cautiously entered the room, his gun ready for anything. He could see Lena on the far wall looking over, trying to pull herself over.

"Ok guys, play time over!" Mark said, as he stepped into the room. "Derrick, you come out of there and be with your girl, that's not exactly where I wanted to bury you."

Misdirection is the key to any surprise. Mark was about to find this out. As Lena slowly turned, her eyes were slightly elevated as though glancing at something on the ceiling.

Mark knew he had been had! He started to spin around, but it was too late! Hit from behind, Mark was thrown to the floor, sending his pistol flying across the room. Derrick had jumped on him from the ledge, just above the door. Wrestling for Mark's gun, the two men rolled on the ground neither getting the advantage.

Lena watched, frozen, not knowing what to do.

Retrieving the gun, Mark bought it to Derrick's chest.

At the last possible second, Derrick deflected the gun, sending it flying, but not before the bullet grazed his side. Derrick felt the burning, but could not evaluate it at this time. Mounting Mark, Derrick came down with two hard elbows on his head, rendering him unconscious.

Getting to his feet, Derrick went to Lena.

"We need to get you to a doctor!" Lena said, the words hardly out of her mouth before the sound of a shovel dragging the ground could be heard.

THE MARDI GRAS MURDERS

Derrick turned to see a shovel coming down toward him. Pushing Lena to the side, Derrick sidestepped the shovel, as it landed hard against the wall. Derrick was almost defenseless now, adrenalin no longer drove him, and the pain from the gunshot had rendered him all but helpless. Mark pulled back the shovel once more, Derrick could do nothing but wait as the shovel came toward him as though it were in slow motion. Then just as the shovel seemed like it was going to find its target, another shovel came out of nowhere and sent Mark flying backward. Derrick looked to his side to see Lena, rearing back for another strike. This one struck Mark on the head, sending him backward toward a mound of dirt, which lined the wall. But Mark would never reach it, as he fell backward a pick ax, which had been haphazardly stuck in the mound, tore through his chest. Mark died with a look of shock and surprise on his face.

Lena turned her attention once more to Derrick.

"Where did you learn to swing like that?" Derrick asked, leaning on Lena, as she led him out.

Latter that day,

Derrick emerged from the hospital just as his brother was driving up.

"You Ok?" he asked, a worried look on his face.

"Yea, I'll be fine, it just grazed me," Derrick explained, easing his brother's concern.

"Well, it looks like you're in some good hands," Bob said, referring to Derrick leaning on Lena. "We picked up what was left of Mark, and I've got men going through his house. We found what you said we would. I would never have suspected him," Bob said. "But you never know what will make a person's mind snap like that. Well, you solved another big case, I guess you got a hero welcome back in Chicago."

THE MARDI GRAS MURDERS

"Well," Derrick said, "I still have some unfinished business here," He looked at Lena with a big smile. Reaching into his pocket, he removed the address to his mother's house that Bob had given him earlier. "How would you like to meet my mom?"

Bob smiled a big smile. "Right this way, folks," he said, as he opened the rear door of his sedan.

This journey had proved far more than Derrick could have ever hoped for. He no longer thought about drowning himself in a bottle. He had found a love, and most of all, he had found his family again. And when all is said and done, in the final analysis, family is all that matters.

THE MARDI GRAS MURDERS

OTHER GREAT TITLES BY
Ricardo S. Dubois

Ghost Squirrel
Swamp Witch
A Time for Miracles
Crossroads
The Treasure of Jean Lafitte
Vengeance is Mine!
Southern Justice
Turnabout
The Mardi Gras Murders
City Beneath the Sea

Autograph copies available by contacting me at:
craftycajun@yahoo.com